# Silent
## Distraction

### Sign of Love Series
### Book 2

## Tonya Clark

# ACKNOWLEDGMENTS

This book is dedicated to my Grandma Blanche, who may no longer be with us, but I know she is smiling down from above. I thank you for introducing me to my first romance novel, even though she had no idea she did at the time. If you wouldn't have left that book in my room when you came to visit, I may never have found a love for reading.

# CHAPTER ONE

Cameron

"Steve, just order what needs to be replaced in the morning. This damn deadline can't be pushed back. This is why I hate track homes. I'll call my dad in the morning and let him know what's going on."

I had told my dad I didn't want to take on this project and these last few months reminded me of why. This is the third time we have had these 'pain in my ass' teenagers come through and break out the windows of the houses. I'm starting to think we need to order more security at night. It would be cheaper to do that than to have to keep replacing all the windows.

"Cam, we need to do something about these..."

My phone beeps through with another call, cutting off

what Steve is saying. The number isn't anyone I recognize. If it is too important, they will leave a message.

Bringing the phone back up to my ear, Steve is still talking. "What are we going to do about these little shits?"

Steve is my right hand man down here in Texas. He is amazing at his job, but the man is going to give himself a heart attack one of these days.

My dad hired him when I told him I wanted to move down here to Texas and expand Tovaren Construction, our family business. Steve and I handle Texas and my dad runs things up there in Washington. It was great for the business, we have been pretty busy north and south.

"I'm going to call the security company tomorrow morning and hire another officer for the evenings. Maybe we will have a better chance of catching them."

Once again, my phone beeps with another incoming call. Same number, but they didn't leave a message last time, so not really in a rush to answer it this time. I am exhausted tonight and don't really want to deal with business right now. They will just have to get the hint and leave a message.

Steve's voice brings me back to our conversation. "I've thought about staying out there myself to catch the little shits."

I laugh, I can see Steve, the 'good ol' country boy' that he is, sitting out there in his truck, his shotgun in his lap. "Steve, you would have way too much fun scaring the crap out of those kids."

"Yes, I would get a little pleasure out of it, but I could guarantee they wouldn't do it again."

"I would love to see it myself, but let's try the extra security first. If that doesn't work, I'll let you loose on them."

Opening my fridge, I find that I'm ordering pizza for dinner tonight. Tomorrow I think I may need to go shopping.

Grabbing one of the last two beers I have, I go and drop down onto the couch.

"Hey, Steve, I'll see you in the morning. I need to order a pizza and then I'm going to bed, I'm exhausted."

"You need a woman. One that knows how to cook. You eat out way too much."

"I don't need a woman who can cook, I can cook for myself. I'm actually a pretty damn good cook, I just need to go shopping for food. We have been so busy lately with finishing this project that I haven't made it to the store."

"Are you still seeing that redhead?"

"Candice? Yeah, off and on, it's nothing serious."

For the third time, my phone beeps through with another call. Same number. Whoever this is isn't giving up. "Hey, someone is trying to get a hold of me, they have called three times now. I should probably see what they want. I'll talk to you tomorrow."

"All right, and just as a reminder, my offer stands to stay on the property one of these nights."

"I'll remember, and I'll keep you posted on what I find out about the extra security. See ya." Hanging up, I find the number and call it back.

It rings a couple times and right when I think it will go to voicemail, a man's voice answers. "Hello."

"Hello. Someone from this number has called me a couple times tonight." That was a lot nicer than I want to be.

"Cameron, is this you?"

"Yes, who is this?"

"I'm glad we finally reached you. Your brother said he texted you but you haven't answered. I'm David Colter. Your brother, Jacob, and my son, Tyler, are good friends."

Pulling my phone away, I find three messages from Jacob

that I haven't read. I remember seeing the first one a little earlier but I figured I'd text him back later. Now I have Tyler's dad calling me. Maybe I shouldn't have ignored them.

"Mr. Colter, I believe we have met before. Is everything all right?"

Something isn't settling right. If something is wrong with Jacob, why aren't my parents calling me?

Silence stretches on the other end of the line. "Mr. Colter, are you still there? Is Jacob all right?"

I hear David clear his throat. "Yes, Jacob is fine. I'm, um..."

I'm starting to get impatient. All my nerves are on alert. Something is wrong, and if it's not Jacob, then there are only my parents.

"Cameron, there isn't an easy way to tell you this. This evening there was an explosion at one of our restaurants and your parents were there during that time."

"Explosion?! What kind of explosion? Are they all right?"

Again, silence. I want to reach through the phone and shake the man.

"Cameron, details haven't really been released yet. Search crews are still looking for survivors, but it's not looking very good."

What does he mean, not looking good for survivors?

"How do you know they were there?"

"Jacob came over tonight to hang out with Tyler. He told us your parents had decided to go out for dinner and asked if he could eat with us tonight. I was watching the television when the news broadcast came over the show I was watching. I asked Jacob which restaurant your parents had gone to and he confirmed the same one."

"Are you sure? Has anyone tried calling them?"

"Yes, Jacob and I have tried a number of times. Neither of them are answering."

Something is wrong then. My dad always answers his phone. He always says, "A missed call is a possible missed customer."

My entire body feels like someone injected ice cold water into my veins.

"How long ago did all this happen? How many times have you tried to call them? Maybe something just happened to their phones."

"Cameron, we have been trying since we heard. It happened around five tonight. Every time we call, both phones go straight to voicemail and none of your brother's messages have been answered back."

Five?! My parents wouldn't go this long without contacting someone after something like this happening.

"I'll be on the first flight I can get. Are you good with Jacob staying there until I can get there?" I feel numb. It all feels like a dream; my parents can't be dead.

"Of course! Call me with your flight information and I'll come pick you up. If we hear anything before then I'll let you know. We left our information with the police when we called earlier."

"Thank you." I hit end without waiting for David to say anything else. I can't move, all I can do is stare down at my phone. This can't be happening. Who the hell blows up a restaurant?

# CHAPTER TWO

Jayden

"All right, guys, time is up for today. If you are still needing help, I'll have another after school session on Wednesday," I sign to the five students who have attended tutoring today.

I watch as they all clean up and start to leave. They each sign thank you as they walk past my desk.

Emily is the last to leave. She waits for everyone to exit and then walks up to my desk. "Ms. Edwards, I want to thank you for all the after school help. I have never been good or liked math. You have changed that. I just wanted to say thank you," she signs.

My heart melts a little. This is why I decided to become a teacher. I had also struggled in math. All it took was one special teacher, Mrs. Morris, my sophomore year math teacher. Because of her, I decided to teach and chose math as well.

"Anytime, Emily! I'm happy it's helping. Your grades are definitely improving. You have a good evening. I'll see you in class tomorrow."

Smiling, she nods and leaves the classroom. Never would I have guessed I would be teaching at a deaf school. I met my best friend, Charliee, who is deaf, my junior year of college. She was in one of my classes with an interpreter. I was extremely fascinated and couldn't stop watching them when they would sign back and forth. It was beautiful to watch.

I have never been shy, and one day after class I ran up to her and introduced myself. After probably a dozen questions, that I shot off so fast I believe the interpreter had a hard time keeping up, we became best friends. Learning sign language seemed to come pretty natural to me. After graduation, we were both offered jobs here at the deaf school. Charliee teaches English and I was offered Math, both of us at the high school level.

Glancing up at the clock, I realize if I don't get moving, I am going to be late for the meeting. Quickly grabbing my purse and bag, I head for the office, locking my classroom door before speed walking to the meeting I was asked to sit in on about Jacob Tovaren.

Jacob is a great kid. Popular, great student academically. He is athletic, loved by all the girls. Tragedy struck his family a couple weeks ago when a popular Italian restaurant was blown up, killing eighteen people. Among those eighteen were both of Jacob's parents.

Charliee was there that night as well. The call I received from her parents that night will forever be burned into my memory. I had just gotten out of the shower and was sitting down to enjoy a little television while grading some papers. I was flipping through the channels, not wanting to watch the news, which seemed to be on every channel. I hate watching the news, it's too depressing.

I had just realized what they were reporting about when my phone rang. It was Charliee's mom, all frantic, asking me if I had seen the news. Charliee had stopped by the restaurant to grab dinner before heading home. She was been leaving the place when the bomb went off. They found her under the fallen building and had just rushed her to the hospital.

Her back was badly burned, she had stitches across one of her shoulders and a broken arm, but she was alive. However, she was still in the hospital recovering from her burns.

Hurrying into the front office, I quickly wave at Cindy sitting at the front desk and rush into the principal's office.

"Sorry I'm late. My tutoring class ran a little over today," I speak and sign as I enter.

"Slow down, Ms. Edwards, and have a seat. We were just about to get started." Mr. Lennerd, the principle, pointed to an empty chair.

Turning around to take my seat, I stumble. There standing against the back wall, arms crossed over his chest, his eyes looking me up and down, is a man I've never seen before.

His mouth slants up at one corner as I quickly regain my balance and take my seat.

"Ms. Edwards, are you all right?" Mr. Lennerd asks, bringing my attention back to him.

"Yes, thank you. I'm fine. Foot just got tangled up." I look over my shoulder, that cocky smile is still there, his eyes are still on me.

"Ms. Edwards, I'd like you to meet Mr. Tovaren," Mr. Lennerd makes the introduction.

"It's nice to meet you, Mr. Tovaren."

He nods, but doesn't move from his spot against the wall. "Call me Cameron. Mr. Tovaren was my father."

My heart skips a little. I'm just not sure if it's from the sound of his smooth voice or the mention of his father.

"I'm sorry for your loss. I met your parents a number of times, they were a very nice couple."

His smile drops, as do his eyes for a moment. I have to fight the urge to go to him and wrap my arms around him. When he looks back up at me, the small smile has returned. It's all for show. I can tell by the sadness in his eyes.

Our eyes stay locked. Nothing is being said, but I feel a pull to this man. It's strange, I have never had this kind of feeling over a guy.

The clearing of a throat pulls me out of my trance and my attention away from the dark-haired god leaning against the wall.

"Sorry, Mr. Lennerd, what were you saying?" I look down at my folder in my lap as I speak, hoping to hide my red cheeks.

What is wrong with me? I don't blush. Guys don't make me react like a high school girl. Embarrassment is a new feeling for me and I'm not liking it at all.

When I glance up at Mr. Lennerd, my cheeks burn a little more. He is giving me a knowing look. To top everything off, I can feel Cameron's eyes on my back. I have to fight the urge to glance back over my shoulder again.

"I was saying that Mr. Tovaren..."

"Cameron," the voice from behind me interrupts Mr. Lennerd.

"I apologize. Cameron has asked for this meeting because Jacob is having some problems with math while he has been out. We had decided, as you know, to put Jacob on home studies for a month while they deal with the family tragedy. Mr..., I mean Cameron, called me yesterday saying Jacob is struggling with math and doesn't want to have him fall too far behind. I figured you being his teacher, and I know you hold study groups for your students pretty frequently, that maybe we can work something out to help him out."

"Ms. Edwards..." The silky voice pours over me as he says my name. What is wrong with me? Damn, I need to pull myself together.

I turn in my chair, facing Cameron again, he hasn't moved a muscle. "Please, call me Jayden. Ms. Edwards is for the children."

His eyes narrow. Yes, Mr. Tovaren, you may have knocked me senseless for a moment but I bounce back quickly. I speak to him with my eyes. I know he understands by those lips curving just a little more, and his eyes accept the challenge.

He may have knocked me off balance for a moment, but I don't stay off kilter for long.

"Jayden..." he continues.

It's a good thing I am sitting because hearing my name with that voice would have had me down on my knees.

"I don't think my brother is ready to be back at school, even if it's after school hours."

"Actually, we were wondering if you could go to the house and tutor him there. That is if you have time," Mr. Lennerd comes into the conversation.

Looking between the two men in the room, I think about it for a moment. It would probably be hard for Jacob to be around all the kids and their questions. They wouldn't mean any harm but they would smother him with it all, and it would definitely be overwhelming for him. I was emotional answering all of their questions about Charliee when it all first happened.

"You are right, coming here would be difficult I'm sure. I have no problem tutoring him at home."

Pulling a business card out of my bag, I grab a pen off the desk and write down my cell phone number. "Here is my cell number, give me a call and we can set up a schedule."

When I turn to hand it to Cameron, he is standing right next to me and my hand smacks into his very hard stomach. "I'm sorry."

His stomach muscles flex under my touch, but when I look up, he looks cool and collected. Very good, Mr. Tovaren, you played it off well. Your face may show no effect from my touch, but your body speaks loud and clear. He is just as affected by me as I am him.

Cameron takes the card from my hand, flipping it over to where I wrote my number. "Thank you. I'll be calling you soon. I don't want Jacob to fall too far behind."

"Your brother is a very smart kid, but he has struggled with math. I'm sure we can get him caught up pretty quickly."

"Thank you." Cameron turns to Mr. Lennerd, "Thank you for your time and help. I'll stay in touch on when Jacob will be coming back to school." The two men shake hands.

"Miss. Edwards, you will be hearing from me soon." I see the smile before he turns from me to leave the office.

"It was nice to meet you, Mr. Tovaren," I say as he reaches for the handle.

He stops for a moment. I think he will say something in return, but instead he leaves the office without saying another word.

Looking over at Mr. Lennerd, I find my cheeks heating up again with the knowing smile he gives me. "What?"

"There won't be any problems with this set up, will there?"

If only he knew how many times I had asked myself that very question in the last few minutes. "Of course not, why would you think there would be?"

Mr. Lennerd just gives me that knowing smile again. Damn, was I that obvious earlier? "It will be fine, Mr. Lennerd. I'll be very professional. Jacob is the most important person involved here. I don't want him falling behind. There will be no issues, I promise."

Mr. Lennerd sits there studying me. Yes, Cameron is a very handsome guy. True, no one has made me want to grab onto them and not let go until we are both naked and exhausted like I felt when he spoke my name. Besides wanting those lips all over my body, I have no other problems. It will all be fine. I give Mr. Lennerd what I hope is a very reassuring smile.

"How is Charliee doing?"

I almost slump back in the chair with relief when he changes the subject.

"She is doing a lot better. They are hoping she can go home in a couple of days."

"That's good, we miss her here. Please let her know we are happy to hear she is healing and can't wait for her to be back in the classroom."

"I'll let her know. See you tomorrow." I grab my bag and head out of the office.

I am very ready to be home and relaxing in my spa. What a day!

# CHAPTER THREE

Cameron

Shutting the door to my dad's truck, a whiff of his smell catches me off guard. I close my eyes, expecting to open them and see him sitting next to me. No one is there, just me, alone, sitting in the parking lot of my brother's school. I need to figure out a way to get my truck up here from Texas and soon.

Turning the key in the ignition, I know I just want to be home. Of course that has nothing but memories either. Before backing out, I catch a glimpse of Ms. Edwards, or should I say Jayden walking through the parking lot.

Instantly my stomach muscles flex again, like they remember her touch. Jayden has fire in her, I could see it in her eyes when she gave me her challenging look earlier. I saw the heat as well. When her hand connected with my stomach and those eyes shot up to mine, desire filled me, and it took everything I had to not grab her hand and pull her up against me. My body wanted to fill more than just her hand. I wanted her body up against mine. Better yet, I would have been good with clearing off that desk and laying her body under my own.

I watch her as she walks across the lot, her eyes down looking at her phone the whole way. She gets to what I figure is her car, gets in and pulls out. Watching her car until it disappears on the street, my stomach jumps again. What the hell is wrong with me? I need to shake this want for Jayden. I don't have time for anything other than running the family business, all the legal matters and my brother.

Jacob and I are eleven years apart. I remember when Mom and Dad told me they were having a baby. Mom was so excited. They had been trying for years. I remember asking why they wanted another kid. Dad smiled and told me, "Don't worry, Cameron, your mom and I have so much love, there is plenty of room for both of you."

Mom just glowed the whole time she was pregnant, even though she had been sick the whole time. I swear she smiled even when she was throwing up every day. Then Jacob was born. They told us he was deaf. As expected, all the attention the new baby received and more because of the added disability, I went through a few years of rebelling.

I didn't spend much time in the first five years with Jacob. Everything changed one night when our family was out to dinner. We had a table next to ours with a couple of older kids with their parents. The kids were making fun of Jacob because of his signing and the sounds he made. I tried to ignore it and could have ignored the ignorance of teenagers, but the father made a comment about my brother being a retard. I told my parents that I had to use the restroom. As I walked by the table, I hooked the father's chair with my foot and pulled it out from under him, sending him and his plate to the floor. I didn't even look back.

The man glared at me as I walked back to our table a short time later. It took a lot to not stop and say something to him as well, but I decided to be satisfied with sending his ass to the ground. Sitting back down, I was expecting the third degree from my parents. Neither of them looked up from their plates, they just sat there eating, but I didn't miss the smiles on their faces.

From that night forward, I made a vow to myself that no one would hurt my little brother, physically or mentally, regardless of what he was aware of. We became attached at the hips after that night. When I decided to move down to Texas three years ago, Jacob tried to talk my parents into letting him move with me. We text almost every day when I'm not homing visiting.

Since our parent's death a couple weeks ago, he hasn't said much to me at all. He eats dinner up in his room. He doesn't go anywhere either. When his friends come over, he sends them away, telling me to tell them he isn't home or busy.

When he had told me he wanted some time off from school, I understood. I didn't see any harm in letting him take a little time away from school as long as he kept up with his work and grades. This might not have been the best idea. I'm starting to think I should have kept him in school.

Living alone in Texas never bothered me. Coming home to a quiet house was relaxing. Coming home to the house I grew up in is a different thing. Standing here on the porch, I almost hate to open the front door. I still expect to hear Mom in the kitchen and see Dad in his office on the phone with a client. Jacob and his best friend Tyler on the couch playing video games. Now all I hear is silence and it isn't relaxing. Eventually I'll get use to this new silence, right?

Shutting the door behind me, I am thrown back a little when I hear a sound coming out of the kitchen. I know it isn't my mom, but damn the memories flood back. Surprisingly I find Jacob looking through the fridge.

I reach around him and grab a beer. I expect him to turn around and acknowledge me, but he doesn't even look over his shoulder. He doesn't talk to me unless I make him.

When he does turn, he doesn't say anything. He begins to walk past me, but I put my hand out and stop him.

"I met with your math teacher today, Miss Edwards," I sign to him.

Still nothing, it is starting to piss me off. "She has agreed to come here to the house and tutor you."

"Okay," he signs back, but that is all. He just stands there giving me the look, like I'm wasting his time.

"Have you done anything today other than sit in your room? Maybe you should see if Tyler can hang out tonight. I'm going to throw some chicken on the barbeque for dinner. Why don't you see if he wants to come over?"

Again, nothing. He just stands against the counter, looking up only to see me sign, then he looks back down at the soda he is holding. I have to fight the urge to throw my hands up in the air and surrender.

"All right, well I'll throw on an extra piece just in case," I sign.

Nothing, Jacob just walks past me and leaves. I have no idea how to handle all of this. I'm supposed to be the older brother, not the parent. There is no manual on what to do with younger siblings after a parent's death.

My phone goes off in my pocket and as irritated as I am

right now, all I want to do is take it out and throw it against the wall. Seeing it is Steve, relief floods through me.

"Hey, Steve."

"Hey, how are things going up there?"

"It's going. I'm trying to stay on top of all the projects Dad had going up here. I don't think the man ever slept. How is the track going?"

"It's on schedule, and since we pulled the extra security for the nights, we have had all the windows staying in one piece."

Well, at least some good news from somewhere. "That's good to hear. Are you able to handle everything all right alone?"

I know that is probably a very stupid question. The man probably knows more than I do.

"Cameron, don't worry about anything on this side of things. Everything is under control and running on time. You, I'm sure have your hands full with things up there in Washington."

Looking around the living room, my chest tightens up. It had always felt good to come home. It was warm, loving, and welcoming. Now it only feels quiet and cold. My hands being full is an understatement. Between Jacob, my father's open jobs, piles of paperwork, and the household affairs, I am in overload. I wonder every day how my parents made this all look so easy.

I know the business, I just never realized how much my dad had taken on up here. I think what is driving me over the edge is Jacob. Being the older brother is one thing; becoming the legal guardian of a teenager who just lost both parents, dealing with all of his school issues and trying to get him to talk to me is a totally different thing.

"Cameron, are you still there?" Steve's voice brings me out of my own head.

"Yeah, sorry. I was thinking."

"Do you need me to come up there and handle the job sites for a couple weeks? I can at least take that load off you for a little bit."

"I appreciate it, Steve, but I need you down there more than up here. I have Kevin helping me out on the sites up here while I get the business side all taken care of. We can't afford for something to go wrong down there with both of us being up here."

"All right, but know if you need me, I'm only a flight away."

"I appreciate that."

"Oh, real quick before I let you go. That little redhead stopped by the job site office the other day looking for you."

"Candice?" How did she even know where the office was?

"I'm assuming you didn't tell her you left."

We had been on a couple dates, we weren't serious. "I've been ignoring all of her calls to be honest. Things up here are a little more important than dealing with her right now. Sorry about that. If I would have thought she'd end up there bugging you, I would have talked to her."

"It's no big deal. I wasn't sure what you had told her, so I just said you weren't in at the time."

"I'll call her later today and let her know I'm not in town. Sorry about that."

"Don't apologize, it's no big deal."

"I should be able to come down for final inspection so I'll see you in a couple weeks."

"Sounds good. I would say try not to stress, but from the sound of your voice I believe you have already passed that."

I didn't respond, I just pressed end and tossed my phone onto the couch next to me, which then bounced onto the floor. Bending down to pick it up, I find a business card on the floor. Picking it up, I realize it is the one Ms. Edwards had given to me earlier, it must have fallen out of my pocket.

That warm feeling spreads through my stomach again. Before I really realize what I am doing, I dial the number on the back of the card. Three rings and I think I will be talking to an answering machine, but I'm surprised when her voice says, "Hello."

"Hello, Ms. Edwards, this is Cameron Tovaren."

Silence stretches out for a moment but then her silky voice comes through the line. "Hello, Mr. Tovaren. I'm a little surprised to hear from you so soon."

My skin usually chills when someone calls me Mr. Tovaren, but I find myself smiling at Jayden using the name for me. She is giving back what I am dealing.

"The longer I wait to get Jacob started with tutoring, the more behind he will be."

"Understandable, when were you thinking of getting started?"

Tonight, in my bed is what I want to answer. "What days do you have available? I'll work about your schedule."

"I can stop by tomorrow after school if that works for you. I can be there around four-thirty."

Jayden's voice is very soothing, I can feel my body relaxing as we talk. I need to figure out how to keep her on the phone. "Four-thirty it is! Do you need me to get anything, supplies or anything?"

I hear a small laugh. "No, we won't need anything. He should have his book."

"Okay, well then I guess we will see you tomorrow."

"Wait! I do need one thing from you."

"What would that be, Ms. Edwards?"

"Your address, Mr. Tovaren." Her voice melts through the phone.

I have never wanted to grab someone and pull them through a phone as badly as I want to at this moment. I have to fight the urge to clear my throat. She would take great pleasure in knowing the affect she is having on me, I have a feeling.

"I'll text it to you when we hang up."

"Sounds good."

"See you tomorrow, Ms. Edwards."

"Mr. Tovaren, I can play this name game as long as you can."

I laugh, something I haven't done in a couple weeks. She is forward, says what she wants. I like that!

"See you tomorrow," she adds.

"Goodbye."

Jayden hangs up the phone first. I sit here staring at mine. I save her name with her number, smiling to myself as I type in Ms. Edwards (Jayden).

# CHAPTER FOUR

Jayden

I'd seen Cameron sitting in his truck in the school parking lot when I came out. I felt his eyes follow me as I walked to my car. It took everything I had in me not to look over at him as I walked past. He had started to back out just as I came out of the building. I would have paid good money to know what he was thinking. Funny thing was, usually when I knew a guy was checking me out, I would make sure he didn't miss a move or sway of my hips. When I saw Cameron and knew that he was watching me, all I wanted to do was run for my car, and not in a sexy way. These weren't feelings I was used to. Never has one touch of a guy made me think about him this much. I don't do the relationship thing. Sure, I go out, we have fun for a couple dates, but then I end things before they get serious. Charliee says it's because of what my dad did to my mom.

I remember thinking I was the luckiest girl in the world. All of my friends would talk about their parent's getting divorces or they were already separated. Having to move between houses, or some would talk about how they never saw one or the other. I would just sit there and think to myself how lucky I was that my parents were still in love with each other. I never heard my parents fight. We always took family vacations together. We were the perfect family. Well, that's what I thought any way.

I remember one evening I found my mom crying in the kitchen. I was thirteen, but it still feels like it was yesterday. My father had decided to cheat on my mom with a lady he worked with, and he left both of us for that family. No warning, he never even said goodbye, he just packed his things and left, leaving my mom a note.

I haven't seen my father since that day. He has tried to reach out to me and my mom has tried to convince me that I should talk to him, but I have no desire to have him in my life. I watched what his actions did to my mom.

Somehow, my mom was able to find love in her heart again for another man. She found Todd. He is a great guy, treats my mom like she is the only woman alive. She deserves someone like him. I'm so happy that she was able to find someone who appreciated her.

I have kind of decided that it isn't worth all the pain. That's why I only date and that's where it stays. I can't get hurt if I don't get too close. I go out, meet a guy, enjoy the evening, a little dancing, a few drinks and that is usually where it ends. A few I have taken it further into the night, or on a couple more dates, but that's it.

Cameron, I haven't stopped thinking about. What the hell is wrong with me? Sure, he's good looking. He has a body I won't deny is built like a god, but he isn't the first guy I've met with those features.

I had just stepped out of the hospital from visiting Charliee when my phone rang. I didn't recognize the number and almost let it go straight to voicemail, but for some reason I answered it. The sound of his voice when he said hello and called me Ms. Edwards almost caused me to melt to the ground there in the hospital parking lot. I thought I was being all clever when I called him Mr. Tovaren back, but he didn't respond. I found myself feeling disappointed, why I don't know. He doesn't seem like the type of guy who jokes around. He did, however, accept challenges, and so did I. If he wasn't going to call me Jayden, then I wasn't going to call him Cameron.

Walking into my house, I go straight back to my room and strip out of my clothes. My hot tub is waiting for me. The warm water is calling my name. This is my daily routine: home, strip, hot tub. When I moved in, I had the patio covered so that I didn't have to worry about giving my neighbors a show.

As I sink down into the water, I can feel all of my muscles relax as the water covers me. This is probably my favorite time of the day. Laying my head back, I close my eyes, sinking lower into the water and letting the heated bliss surround my entire body up to my chin. It feels amazing. Why am I so tense tonight? Classes went well. Charliee is doing great, maybe a little stir crazy, but healing fast.

Cameron, leaning up against the wall, arms crossed over his chest and a small sexy smile. This is what I see when I close my eyes, and my body tenses right back up. I can feel my body heat up, and I'm pretty sure it's not from the water I'm sitting in.

Charliee had even asked me today why I was so tense. That woman picks up on everything, damn her for being deaf. Not being able to hear heightened all of her other senses.

Charliee has felt so guilty about being one of the survivors, and all the people who lost their lives. Especially Mr. and Mrs. Tovaren. It is hitting her hard. When she asked about my day, I didn't want to mention Cameron. I was afraid it would dampen her mood today.

What did I really have to tell her anyway? We met for what, a whole ten minutes? Which is one of the reasons it is driving me crazy that I am having the feelings that I'm having. Thinking about going to the house tomorrow and tutoring Jacob isn't helping my nerves either. All right, this hot tub isn't doing the job tonight. I've never wanted to slap myself in the face before and tell myself to get a grip.

My phone goes off with a text message. It is probably Charliee. She has nothing else to do all day except text me. Most of the time it is just little text messages, like come break me out of jail.

This water isn't helping. Actually it is getting a little hot in here, almost smothering. I didn't grab anything on the way home for dinner, which I could smack myself for forgetting. I don't have much in the way of food here at the house. I need to go shopping, but when? Between work, after school tutoring, and visiting Charliee, there isn't much time left in the day, but I am going to have to find it somewhere.

Jumping out of the hot tub, I grab a towel, wrapping it around me as I head back into my room and to the kitchen, grabbing my phone off my bed as I go. Expecting Charliee's name, I stumble when I see Cameron's. It is the text giving me his address.

Going off once again as I am reading that text, I almost throw the phone down the hallway when Cameron's name shoots across the screen.

**Do you prefer I'm home when you come over tomorrow?

Now that could be a loaded question. One side of me wants to play with it a little, the other side, however, the professional side decides on keeping it clean.

**I think a guardian present is the best idea please.

His response comes back quickly.

**All right, see you tomorrow then.

I find myself smiling down at the phone and Cameron's last text. This is so wrong, I'm acting like a high school girl with a crush on the popular guy, who just said hello to me. I'm not in high school. I don't have a crush. I'm a grown damn adult with a job to do and I need to get my head on straight. Damn you, Cameron Tovaren!

Another text message comes through, this one scaring the hell out of me and causing me to jump, my phone flying out of my hands and landing hard on the floor. I swear out loud and then chant to myself, "Please don't be broken. Please don't be broken," as I pick it up.

The breath I am holding rushes out when I flip it over and find everything all good. The screen isn't cracked. Enough is enough, I have to stop thinking about Cameron. This is insane.

I open the screen, expecting to see Cameron's name, but I'm relieved when it is from Charliee.

**I know you were just here, but I love you tons!!

I love this girl. I can only imagine what she is wanting me to do.

**I love you too. What do you want?
**A hamburger and fries!!!

Another message follows it with a picture of what I think may be her dinner that the hospital is trying to get her to eat. I can't make out what it is supposed to be. Underneath the picture she wrote, "I'm begging."

Perfect, now I can grab her and me something to eat.

**Give me half an hour. I'll even go and get our favorite.
**You are the best, I owe you big time.

If anything, I owe her. She is giving me an excuse to go out and maybe that will take my mind off Cameron. I wish I could talk to her about all of it really. It feels a little strange not to say anything to her, we tell each other everything. This is different though. She needs to heal and get over this guilt she's feeling. Talking about the Tovaren family won't help her with that. Plus, there isn't anything to really tell her yet.

# CHAPTER FIVE

Cameron

The doorbell rings and all the lights begin to flash. Looking at the clock, it is four-twenty. "That is probably Ms. Edwards," I sign to Jacob.

He nods slightly and then looks back down at whatever school work he is working on. Frustrated, I get up from my dad's desk where I have been working on paperwork most of the afternoon and head to the door.

The doorbell rings once again before I reach it. Opening the door, my stomach tightens. She is dressed pretty simple. Tight jeans and a button-up shirt, but those red boots are what catches my attention.

"Are you a Footloose fan?"

Jayden looks down at her boots, a small smile on her lips

when she looks back up at me. "I could say I like to express my rebel side a little, but red is my favorite color and I've always had a little country girl in me."

*I think I believe the rebel part more than the country girl part,* I think to myself.

"I see, so you are telling me you are a city girl that likes to pretend to be a country girl?"

Her eyes narrow at me, she is trying to read me. Good luck with that, Ms. Edwards. Her eyes roam down my body, down to my boots.

She points down at my boots. "Do you think living in Texas for a couple years makes you a country boy?"

"I found out very quickly how comfortable they are. The country music, however, had to grow on me."

Jayden stands there staring at me for a moment, her eyes searching my face. I have no idea what she is looking for and then finally, she breaks her silence.

"Is Jacob home?"

Nodding, I step to the side so that she can come in. "Come on in, Ms. Edwards."

"Thank you, Mr. Tovaren," she throws back at me as she walks past. I don't miss the little smile either.

She walks right into the living room where Jacob is sitting. She signs something but I can't see what. What shocks me is that Jacob responds, and not just a one word answer. They are having a conversation with each other.

I watch as Jacob gives Jayden a small smile and then gets up from the couch, grabbing all of his books. He walks into the dining room, setting everything down onto the kitchen table, then runs up the stairs.

Looking over at Jayden, I'm sure the question is written all over my face.

"He forgot his math book in his room. If you are good with it, we will work at the dining room table, it'll be easier."

When I don't respond, she rolls her eyes and starts to walk past me. My hand goes to her stomach, stopping her before she can get too far. Electricity shoots through my hand, up my arm, right into my chest. I look down at her, she is looking down at her stomach and my hand. My breath catches when her eyes find mine again.

"Is it not all right if we use the dining room table?" she asks me, her eyes questioning me.

I can't move, or maybe I don't want to move. "He talked to you!" It isn't a question.

Her eyes go from questioning to surprise. "Was he not supposed to?"

I have a need to move my hand from her stomach to her waist and pull her in closer against me. I want her lips. What the hell? Quickly, I remove my hand from her altogether and take a large step away from her.

"Of course you can use the table." I answer the first question, but ignore the last question about Jacob talking to her.

Turning, I head back to the office. "I'll be in the office if you need me," I throw over my shoulder as I walk away. I don't look back at her, I can't.

Sitting down at my father's desk, I find myself staring straight at her, our eyes locked. She hasn't moved since I walked away. She just stands there, looking over her shoulder staring at me. This is crazy. I didn't need, nor did I have the time for any of this. But, here we are, staring each other down and all I want to do is grab her, strip her out of everything except those red cowboy boots, and have her on this desk. My saving grace is hearing Jacob run back down the stairs. It pulls me out of my own thoughts.

Jayden blinks a couple times, then looks away from me and over to Jacob. She signs something to him, that again, I can't see with her back to me, and then they both go and sit down at the table.

Jacob has probably said more to Jayden in the past fifteen minutes that she has been here than he has to me since I have been back home. Which just has me believing that he isn't talking to me for a reason. I still have no idea what it is that he is upset with me on, and I have no idea how to find out if he isn't staying in a room with me longer than he has to.

I've no idea how long I have been sitting here staring at the ordering form that I am supposed to be working on, but I'm sure it's been a while. Every time I go to write something down I find myself staring at the back of the woman sitting in the dining room.

What is it about Jayden that is pulling me toward her this much? Sure, she is beautiful, but I've dated beautiful women before. Although those challenges she is always dealing out with her eyes is something new. Most women I've dated say what they think I want to hear, and I'm not one of those guys that shows affection easily. I like to go out on dates, spend a little time with a pretty female, but I have a business to run, I don't have a lot of alone time to have a serious relationship with one person. Steve laughs at me all the time, saying that the women I date are determined to be the one who catches and breaks me. Then he tells me I'm going to fall hard one day. A woman is going to drop me to my knees.

My eyes adjust to the paper in front of me again. I don't have time for all of this. I need to get my head wrapped around what's important. I have the whole business to run now, not just the Texas side of it. *I don't need a woman in my life right now*, I keep repeating to myself.

My phone vibrates with an incoming call, Candice's name appears. Talk about not having time for a woman. I almost push end to ignore the call, but it isn't fair for Steve to have to deal with her stopping by the office at the work site.

"Hello, Candice."

"Cameron, are you home yet?" She is whining, I can't stand when women whine and pout. How didn't I see all of this back home?

"No, and I probably won't back for some time."

"But I miss you."

Miss me, really? We have only been out a couple times, she acts like we have been in a long-term relationship or something. Now that I have her on the phone and I'm listening to her, I'm trying to figure out how I dealt with all the whining and that squeaky voice at all. I find myself starting at Jayden's back again. She doesn't seem like the whining type. Or the type that would beg for a man's attention.

"Cameron, are you listening to me?" Candice's high-pitched voice breaks into my thoughts.

I take a deep breath. "Yes, Candice, I'm listening. I can't tell you when I'm going to be home."

She doesn't need to know the details of everything going on. "Please don't bug Steve at the office anymore either."

"You aren't going to tell me what's going on? Why you are out of town?"

I need to end this conversation with her. Before I do a very rude thing and hang up on her. "No, I'm not. It's a family concern."

Silence stretches over the lines for a moment. I am starting to think she may have hung up on me.

"Well, call me when you get back in town."

I am a little shocked that this is going to end that easily.
I'm not going to push my luck though.

"Bye, Candice."

"Bye, Cameron." She hangs up quickly.

# CHAPTER SIX

Jayden

A city girl pretending to be a country girl. He thinks he knows me so well. A part of me wants to tell him how much more of a country girl I am, that I didn't grow up in this city life, but he can go on thinking whatever he wants to about me. I'm just here to help Jacob, not impress his older brother.

When his hand made contact with my stomach and I looked up into those chocolate brown eyes, it took everything in me not to jump into his arms, wrap my legs around his waist and take his lips. When he finally moved away from me, I realized I had been holding my breath. I had to take a couple deep breaths as I watched him walk away from me. Then he turned and our eyes locked again. There he was standing behind the desk and I would swear I saw the want in his eyes.

I found myself wanting to follow him in there, clear off the desk and have him take me right there.

Thankfully Jacob came back down the stairs right then, it brought me back to reality and the real reason I was here—to help Jacob, not dream about Cameron. I had to keep reminding myself.

I purposely sit in the chair where my back is to Cameron. I don't need the distraction. Although the whole time I have been sitting here I've gotten the feeling someone is watching me. I can feel Cameron's eyes on my back. I keep wanting to turn around and see if I am right, but I need to pay attention to my job.

My attention is drawn away from my work once again when I hear him answer his phone and say the name Candice, but the rest of the conversation I can't make out. His voice lowers a little and my attention is brought back to Jacob when he taps me on the arm to ask me a question. If Cameron has a girlfriend back home, then I need to stay clear of him altogether.

I catch myself rubbing my stomach as I wait for Jacob to work out the problem we are working on. My skin still feels warm and a little shaky inside from his touch. No one's touch has ever left a feeling behind, a reminder that they had their hands on me.

This isn't staying clear of him, if all I am going to do is think about him the whole time. I'm not going to put myself in the position where I become the other woman. I won't be the cause of some other woman going through the hurt that my mom went through when my dad left her for the "other woman."

Jacob's hands moving bring my attention back again. "Am I doing something wrong?"

"Why do you ask that?" I sign back with a puzzled look on my face.

"You are shaking your head no. I thought you were telling me I was doing it wrong," he explains, signing back to me.

Damn, I got caught not paying attention. "No, you are doing great. Sorry, I was thinking to myself."

Jacob just gives me a small nod and then continues on with his work. I want to slap myself across the face, but I know that would only draw more attention to myself. I really want to turn around and yell at Cameron to stop. Then I think better of that, what if I am only imaging him staring at me? I can see it now. I throw myself around, yelling at him to stop staring and he is not looking at me at all, or he has left the office. Or better yet, he is still on the phone with his girlfriend and she hears me yell and then that starts a problem. The man has a girlfriend, he probably has absolutely no interest in me and I have just wanted him to. That just makes me sound pathetic.

How the hell is one guy's touch making me go this crazy? Enough is enough, no more ideas, dreams, or fantasies of Cameron Tovaren.

Jacob pushes his paper toward me to check the problems he has been working on. *This is why I'm here, to help Jacob while he is out of school*, I remind myself once again. These two men just lost their parents and Charliee is going to need me more after she gets out of the hospital. I have absolutely no time for school girl day dreams, or woman fantasies.

"They are all correct," I sign to Jacob after correcting all his problems.

He gives me a small smile and pulls his paper back. My heart breaks. I've known Jacob for a while now. In school he was always so full of life. Smiling all of the time. The girls in the school followed his every move. He was on the football team and our school track team.

The small smile he just gave me isn't the same guy, it is full of sadness. I hate seeing all of the happiness gone in his eyes. There is none now, it is completely gone. A forced smile at that. I just want to wrap my arms around him and let him know he has someone to talk to if he needs it, but I think that might make him uncomfortable.

Earlier Cameron had seemed surprised when Jacob talked to me. Well, he didn't really talk to me, he answered the questions that I asked him. It almost seemed like Jacob and he weren't talking at all from what I would guess by his surprise. On the other hand, Cameron doesn't seem like the type of guy who would sit down and let you pour your feelings out to either. Most men seem to be uncomfortable with that kind of stuff, women are usually better in that department I think.

Sitting back in my chair, I watch as Jacob works on the last couple math questions. I wonder if there are any females, aunts, sisters, grandmothers that are around or is it just Cameron and Jacob now?

Jacob pushes his paper toward me once again to check the problems he has finished. I quickly run through them.

"I think you have it," I sign and offer him a smile.

Jacob nods and signs, "Thank you," then starts gathering his books and gets up from the table.

I stop him before he can walk away. "I hope I'm not stepping over any lines, but if you need someone to talk to or anything else, I'm a great listener."

I just sit here watching and waiting as he looks down at the floor. When he looks at me again, my heart shatters. His eyes are glassed over from the tears he won't allow to flow. It is everything I can do not to jump out of my chair and hug this poor kid.

"Thank you, but I'm okay," he signs and then quickly leaves the room, running up the stairs.

I am fighting the tears myself now. He has just lost both of his parents in a senseless incident. He isn't all right, he is hurting and probably very confused. His parents dying wasn't an accident, it was by some crazed man who decided to take the lives of innocent people.

Every time I think about the bastard, I want to find him and beat him. My best friend's life will never be the same, but at least she is alive. Jacob and Cameron's life will never be the same and their parents are gone. I can't imagine what I would have done if Charliee wouldn't have survived.

"Why is Jacob upset?" Cameron's voice booms from behind me.

I jump and quickly stand up. I feel like a kid that just got caught doing something sneaky. I turn and find him storming toward me from the office. When he reaches me, he stops only inches away. Fire is in his eyes when he looks straight down at me. Our chests touch every time we both take a breath, that's how close he is standing.

Nothing is said, we just stare each other down. Daring the other one to be the one to back down. I can't do this, all I want to do is grab the front of his shirt and pull his lips down to mine. Now more pissed off at myself for wanting him than at him for accusing me of upsetting Jacob, I quickly turn and begin placing all my stuff in my bag.

I've only grabbed one book when Cameron grabs my arm, turning me back around to face him. Before I can tell him where I think he can go, his lips claim mine. My knees buckle, his arms going around my waist to hold me up at the same time my hand grabs the front of his shirt to keep myself from hitting the floor. My shock quickly wears off and I find myself kissing him back. I want to climb up his body. His body is now pressed completely against mine, it feels like fire is running through all of my veins. I have a need that can't be described.

Then like cold water is splashed over me, the name Candice flashes through my head. I shove myself from him by his chest, breaking the kiss. I take a step back, hitting the table. My legs feel a little wobbly still so I grab onto the table to hold myself up. My lips still feel his and are begging me to go back to kissing him. Neither of us say a word, we just stare at each other, both of us trying to catch our breath.

After a couple deep breaths, when I am sure that I can let go of the table and hold myself up with my own two legs, I quickly turn, grab the rest of my stuff and shove it into my bag. I can't look at Cameron when I turn back around, I just walk past him and out the front door. I don't even bother to close the door behind me. I need to get out of the house and as fast as I can. I'm not even sure if I even take another breath until I get to my car. Throwing my bag into the passenger seat, I slam my door and start my car. Now I am pissed and turned on. Not two feelings that go well together for me.

I jump when my phone goes off with a text message in my pocket. Pulling it out, I see Charliee's name appear on the screen.

**Are you coming by today?

Crap, I have gone and seen Charliee every day since she has been in the hospital. I had planned to stop by for a while after I was done tutoring Jacob, but now all I want to do is go home and hide.

**Sorry, I'm not going to make it tonight.

I feel like the worst best friend right now, but Charliee reads me too well and I don't have it in me to explain tonight.

**Are you all right?
**Yes, just tired. I had a late tutoring.

I even add a happy face hoping she will accept it and not ask any other questions.

**All right, see you later, get some rest. Love ya.

Worst best friend in the world.

**Love you too.

I text back and then throw my phone onto the passenger seat. When I look up, there is Cameron, standing in the front doorway staring at me.

I sit here for a moment just staring back at him. Neither one of us tries to hide from the other. He doesn't look cocky at the moment either, which I find is his usual expression. The man pours with confidence, he is usually pretty sure of himself I feel. Right at this moment, though, he looks everything but confident. Usually I would say I have the same confidence in myself, but around Cameron I'm not sure of anything.

The name Candice flashes in my head once again. The

heat in my body quickly cools. I don't know who she is, but I wouldn't be surprised if Cameron has a girlfriend. I feel almost sick right now. If he does have a girlfriend and he just kissed me...anger begins to take over the passionate feelings. This is a perfect reminder of why I don't get involved, men are not to be trusted!

# CHAPTER SEVEN

Cameron

What the hell was I thinking? I'd say I wasn't thinking at all when I kissed Jayden. I had just come out of the office and was heading in to see how much longer they had so that I knew when I could start dinner, when Jacob ran up the stairs. He didn't look mad, but I could tell something was bothering him.

When I asked Jayden and she spun on me as fast as she did, I was ready for the battle, but with us standing that close, and the fire in her eyes challenging me, I couldn't help myself. I felt her legs give out and that only gave me the perfect excuse to wrap my arms around her waist and pull her tighter against me. When she grabbed the front of my shirt, I about lost myself. She was holding on as though I was her life support.

Her lips were soft and her kiss was hungry. I don't think I have ever wanted a woman as much as I wanted Jayden just from one kiss.

When she pushed away from me and I saw the disgusted look on her face, it felt like cold water had just been dumped on me. I would put money on the fact that the look wasn't because of the kiss. There for a moment she was just as hungry for me as I was for her. Something else happened to put that look in her eyes. It's the same look I'm getting right now from her as she stares at me from her car.

For a moment when she looked up and saw me in the doorway, I would have sworn I saw the want in her eyes, but it changed to the disapproving look so fast, I'm not sure. It is almost like she is judging me. I'm not the only one who was kissing the other. Sure, I may have made the first move and kissed her first, but she was just as affected as I had been. So why she would judge me and give me that look and not take some of the responsibility is beyond me. Maybe she has a boyfriend. I wouldn't know that though. Maybe she is mad because I did kiss her and she liked it, and if she is in a relationship with someone then being mad at me would be easier for her than to be mad at herself and think she did anything wrong. She could have pulled away, or stopped me altogether. Now I am pissed. Quickly, I turn away from her judging eyes and close the door. I need to check on Jacob.

I take the stairs two at a time and when I get to Jacob's room, I'm not surprised to find the door closed. Staring at it, I try to decide if I should go in or not. When Jacob was old enough to need his privacy, my parents told him if his door was closed they knew not to go in, but if it was open at all they knew they could enter. My dad always said if for any reason he thought Jacob was hiding anything, he had the right to enter at any time.

Jacob was never a problem child. Neither one of us were. We had no reason to sneak things around, our parents were always pretty open and forward with us. I think we both knew it would be Mom we had to deal with and we knew her wrath was much worse than Dad's. Mom never yelled or lost her temper, she always stayed calm, and that's probably what scared us the most. Seeing disappointment in her eyes would have been the worst punishment for me I believe.

I have probably been standing in front of Jacob's closed door for five minutes before I decide that he can't keep hiding himself away in his room like he has been doing. Dad wouldn't have allowed it and neither am I anymore.

Opening the door, I find Jacob laying on his bed. I walk over to stand beside the bed. He doesn't even look at me, he just keeps his eyes up toward the ceiling. If he thinks ignoring me will have me just walk back out, he is wrong. I will stand here until he decides to look at me.

"My door was closed," he finally signs, but still doesn't look at me.

So I wait a little longer. After a couple more minutes, his eyes find mine. My heart slams in the back of my chest. His eyes are red, it looks as though he has been crying.

"I noticed something was wrong when you passed me. You want to talk about it?" I sign, trying to pull myself together.

He doesn't answer back, he just stares at me. "Look, you have been moping around long enough, Jacob. You need to get out, see your friends. Maybe it's time for you to go back to school."

The shift in his eyes is very noticeable, he is mad now. Too bad, if I need to push him a little, I will. I would rather push him than allow him to lay here all the time and get lost altogether.

He doesn't say anything. He just gets up from the bed and walks past me to his door. He is waiting for me to leave. Again, he is pushing me out. This is crazy, does he think this is something only he is going through? I don't know what to do anymore. I can't force him to talk to me.

"Fine, stay up here alone. Keep pushing everyone away," I sign as I walk past him and out of the room.

I stop right outside the door, looking back at him. "Dinner will be ready in about an hour."

I don't wait for a response this time. I turn and walk down the hall. Hearing his door close is like a kick in the chest. Before you head down our stairs, my mom had all of our family pictures displayed on the wall. The one I focus on, Jacob had to have been about seven years old, I was seventeen. We were all smiling, but my mom's smile seemed to radiate past ours. She was proud of her men. I'm sure right now she isn't very proud of the way I am handling everything. I am failing with my brother. I can almost see the one look I never wanted to see in my mom's eyes when she looked at me —disappointment!

Pain shoots through my hand and up to my elbow as my fist creates a hole in the wall right next to that family picture.

---

"Cameron, everything is going great. We are right on track and the final inspection is scheduled for two weeks from today. Hiring the extra security worked, like we talked about before. We haven't had any problems. I still think you should have given me one night though. I would have been just as effective and cost a lot less." Steve laughs on the other end of the line.

"Sorry, Steve, I couldn't risk losing you because their parents pressed charges because of your scare tactics."

Flexing my hand, it is still pretty sore. It has been over a week, maybe I should go and have it checked out.

"Please, they wouldn't have said anything or they would have had to tell their parents why they got in trouble to begin with."

Jayden's laughter in the dining room catches my attention. I don't hear anything else that Steve is saying.

I get up from the desk and walk out to the living room where I can see into the dining room clearly, seeing both Jacob and Jayden.

Jayden has been back a few times since we kissed that first night. She usually doesn't say more than she needs to when I'm around. Basically she answers my questions and tells me when the next time she will be here. That is the end of any conversation between us.

I can see them signing back and forth but Jayden's back is to me like always. She always sits in the chair where her back is to me from where I usually stay in the office while she works with Jacob. Jacob is smiling. I haven't seen him smile since I've been home.

"Cameron, are you still there?" Steve's voice breaks into my thoughts.

"Sorry, Steve. Yes, I'm still here."

Jayden spins around, hearing my voice behind her. Jacob's smile quickly vanishes when he realizes I am here. Damn, I don't understand why he is so mad at me.

"Steve, let me call you back."

"Everything all right?"

Is everything all right? *Hell no, nothing is all right,* I want to say.

"Yeah, everything is fine. I just need to call you back." I decide to go with that instead.

"Not a problem." You can tell in Steve's voice he isn't buying the whole everything is fine thing, but he is being the great guy I know and not asking anymore questions. "I'll talk to you later."

I hang up from Steve and notice Jayden signing to Jacob. "We are good for tonight. I'll see you on Thursday."

Jayden is gathering her stuff as quickly as she can. Jacob is following with all of his books. Like always, he doesn't even look at me. He just walks right past me and up the stairs.

"I'll be back on Thursday," Jayden repeats to me, but she won't make any eye contact.

"Jayden, we need to talk, please." We need to clear the air between us, this silent treatment from everyone right now is starting to drive me crazy.

"There really isn't much to talk about. Jacob is doing great, he is getting all caught up with math. He should be fine when he gets back to school."

Jayden isn't looking at me as she speaks to me, which is driving me a little crazy.

"I'm happy to hear all of that, but that's not what we need to talk about.'

Shaking her head, Jayden turns to leave. "There really isn't anything else that needs to be discussed. I'm here to tutor your brother and that's all, Mr. Tovaren."

It's the Mr. Tovaren thing again, is it? I grab her hand and spin her back to me before she can walk away from me.

"Jayden, I want to apologize."

She just stands there not looking at me, her head is bent down, but she isn't pulling away from me either.

"Please, Jayden, I don't want this to continue being uncomfortable between the two of us."

It takes another minute or so, but she finally looks up at me. Fire is in her eyes, she is pissed.

"Like I said, there isn't anything to talk about. It's in the past, a mistake, we move on."

"Move on? You won't even look at me when I talk to you, Jayden, this is crazy. I didn't mean to piss you off when I kissed you. I'm sorry, trust me, it won't happen again."

She pulls her hand back from mine. I don't want to let go but I am trying to make things right, not piss her off more, so I let go.

"Cameron, you kissing me isn't want pissed me off if you want me to be honest."

All right, now I am confused. "Then what pissed you off?"

"Let me take that back. Yes, you kissing me pissed me off."

Now I am really confused, either I pissed her off because I kissed her or not. She takes a deep breath, I can tell she wants to say more.

"Come on, Jayden, tell me what this silent treatment is all about."

"Who's Candice?" she finally blurts out.

I'm sure she can see the surprise written all over my face. How does she know about Candice?

"I heard you talking to her on the phone last week."

She answers the question without me asking more. She shows no embarrassment about asking about my personal life, I like that. No games, which is a refreshing difference.

"So, you do have a girlfriend!"

It isn't a question, she is stating the fact to me. I almost laugh, but the seriousness in her eyes keeps me from it, so I just shake my head.

"Candice isn't my girlfriend, Jayden. I'm not going to tell you we didn't go out a couple of times, but nothing more."

She doesn't say anything, she just stands there studying me. She is searching for something to tell her if I am telling her the truth or not. Then it hits me, she isn't pissed that I kissed her.

"So you're telling me you weren't upset that I kissed you, you were upset because you thought I had a girlfriend when I kissed you?"

"Not that you just had a girlfriend, but that you kissed me while having a girlfriend back home."

Ahh, so that's what this has been all about. "Jayden, I promise you that I don't have a girlfriend. Candice is just a woman who thinks we are more, and is not getting the hint."

A small smile appears on her lips and I am finding myself having to fight the urge to grab and kiss her again. She might not be mad at me any longer, but I don't want to push my luck this quickly.

"You got Jacob to smile today!"

Shock fills her eyes.

"It's been three weeks and he won't even talk to me. He might answer a question and even that is not guaranteed. You not only get him to talk to you, but he was smiling today."

She shrugs, "We were talking about something that happened in class today."

"Would you like to go and grab something to eat, maybe a drink?"

"Mr. Tovaren, are you asking me out on a date?"

I can't fight the need to touch her any longer, I grab her hand again. This little last name game is doing something to me. How is it when someone else calls me Mr. Tovaren my skin crawls, but when Jayden's says it I want to grab her and carry her up to my room?

"Call it what you would like, Ms. Edwards. I just need some time with someone who will talk to me. Maybe you can tell me how to get through to my brother."

She nods, but says nothing else. She just gives me that smile and I swear it is doing things to me.

"Let me order Jacob a pizza and then let him know we are leaving."

# CHAPTER EIGHT

Jayden

I watched as Cameron walks away into the other room, the phone up to his ear ordering pizza for Jacob. This is a surprising twist of the day. If someone would have told me I would be going on a dinner date with Cameron Tovaren tonight, I would have laughed in their face.

My phone goes off in my bag. Pulling it out, I see Charliee's name on the screen. Crap, I'm supposed to go over to her house tonight. She was released from the hospital last Friday. Her parents, brothers, and myself tried to convince her to stay at her parent's house for a few weeks, but she wasn't having any of it, she wanted to be home. I love the woman, but she is so determined to be independent and so against asking or accepting any help, she drives me crazy sometimes.

**Are you still coming over tonight?

Great, what am I supposed to do now? My best friend needs me, but I saw the look in Cameron's eyes when he was telling me about Jacob's distance right now, he needs someone to talk to.

**Is there anyone there with you right now?
**My mom will be here in about ten minutes. She is bringing dinner.

I feel a little better knowing she won't be alone.

**Do you mind if I skip tonight?

I am feeling like the worst friend in the world right now. Charliee needs me, but she isn't going to be alone. Cameron, right now, has no one.

**Is everything all right?

Her next text comes through. I hate that she worries about me, she has enough on her own plate right now.

**Yes, everything is fine. I just forgot about something I had to do.

I'm not used to all this side stepping with Charliee. We usually tell each other everything, but right now, there isn't really a lot to tell.

**Okay, I'll see you later, have a good evening

I will make this up to her tomorrow. She will understand, because I know my friend so well. I know if I were to tell her what is going on, she would tell me to go with Cameron. Charliee never thinks of herself, she always puts other people first.

"Is everything all right?"

Cameron's voice comes from the stairs. I look up and smile.

"Yep, everything is fine. I just had to rearrange some plans."

"If you already had plans for tonight, I understand, Jayden. We can do this some other time."

Shaking my head, I reassure him. "No, everything is fine."

"All right, if you're sure then we can get going. I already told Jacob I was leaving and that the pizza would be here in about thirty minutes."


"I'm not sure if I've said this yet, but thank you for coming over and helping Jacob."

I watch as Cameron plays with the bottle of beer he is holding.

"I'm a teacher, this is what we do."

"House calls aren't in the job subscription."

"Cameron, my job subscription is to teach children. There is no certain location, it doesn't say only in school or a classroom."

"Why can't you just let me say thank you?"

"You're welcome. Are you and Jacob close?"

I watch as he finishes his beer.

"We were, yes. We texted every day when I moved down to Texas. He tried to convince my parents to let him move with me, of course my mom wasn't having that. Things have been a lot different since losing Mom and Dad, though. He won't look at me most of the time."

The sadness in his eyes has me fighting my own tears. I don't know how far I should go with questions into his and Jacob's relationship. Or what questions won't be crossing the line to ask since I really don't know Cameron too well.

"I can't imagine any of this is very easy for either one of you. Do you guys have any other family?"

He nods, but still keeps his eyes downcast. "We have our grandparents on my mom's side. Some aunts and uncles, a couple cousins."

"Do they live close?"

Again, he nods. "We have an aunt and uncle here in Washington, but mostly everyone else is spread out over the states. My grandparents tried getting me to send Jacob to them down in California but I'm not uprooting my brother. His school and friends are here. Plus, neither one of them really sign a whole lot."

"That would make things for Jacob and them very difficult. Jacob can read lips well, but his speech isn't the greatest."

"I wouldn't send him off to family anyway. Don't get me wrong, there have been quite a few times in the last few weeks I wonder if he would be better with someone else since I'm obviously doing something wrong. But, I couldn't let him go to family. He is the only family I have left. We only have each other."

Seeing Cameron like this is a little shocking. The guy hasn't shown an ounce of emotion since knowing him. Now here he sits, looking like a lost little boy. I want to wrap my arms around him and tell him everything will be all right.

"Today, seeing him laugh with you was great. He hasn't

cracked a smile since everything happened. On the other side of it, I feel like I must be doing something wrong."

"Cameron, you aren't doing anything wrong."

He only looks at his empty beer bottle, a look of defeat in his eyes.

"Have you tried sitting down and talking to him about all of this?"

I jump when he slams his beer bottle down on the table, his hands flying up in the air.

"Of course."

"Sorry."

"For what?"

"For upsetting you, that wasn't what I was trying to do," I defend myself.

"You didn't upset me, Jayden, I'm sorry. I'm just frustrated right now. I don't know what to do anymore."

*Is he asking me for advice or is he just needing someone to talk to,* I wonder to myself. We sit in silence for a few moments. He still looks everywhere other than at me. Finally, Cameron breaks the silence.

"So how did you decide to become a teacher in a deaf school? Is someone deaf in your family?"

A change of topic, that is fine with me.

"Actually, I met my best friend, Charliee, in college, she is deaf. When I saw her signing in class one day with her interpreter, I was fascinated. It was beautiful to watch. We became friends and I asked her to teach me sign language. I picked it up pretty quickly. I've wanted to be a teacher since my sophomore year of high school. My teacher for math of all things helped me with that decision. Charliee and I graduated and the deaf school was hiring, somehow we both got jobs, it was meant to be."

"That's quite a story. So you and Charliee are pretty close?"

I nod. A minute ago, I was thankful for the change of subject, now I'm thinking not so thankful. I'm pretty sure he has heard about a teacher from the school being involved within the bombing. He just probably doesn't recognize her by the name.

"Does she teach math as well?"

I shake my head no. I know he is going to figure this out in a minute. I'm not hiding it, but his mood was beginning to improve. I know the moment this topic goes back around to that night, his mood will disappear again.

"She teaches English."

I wait and watch as the realization hits him. I know the moment he figures it out, you can see it written all over his face and body.

"There was an English teacher from the school that was there the night of the bombing."

"Yes, there was. She actually just got released from the hospital a few days ago."

He doesn't ask, he doesn't need to. I see the question on his face and I'm pretty positive he reads the answer on mine.

"How is she?" He finally breaks the silence.

His tone is sharp, almost resentful. That causes very mixed emotions in me. One side of me wants to ask why he asked if he doesn't seem to really care about the answer. The other side doesn't blame him, when he lost both parents that night.

"She's healing slowly but doing well. She has major burns across her lower half of her back, stitches along one whole shoulder and a broken arm. Some bruised ribs, but all in all she is good. She is strong, she's a fighter and hates having people take care of her, so I believe she will be back on her feet and back to school teaching in no time."

Cameron looks lost in thought.

"Cameron, maybe it would help if you talked about what's on your mind."

"There isn't enough hours in a day to tell you everything on my mind these days."

I can only imagine. His life was turned upside down.

"I have nowhere to be if you need to get some stuff out."

Nothing, again he just sits there staring at an empty bottle.

"Maybe talking to someone who understands a little from that night will help."

Cameron's eyes shoot up to mine, then they narrow on me. "Are you trying to tell me you understand what I'm going through, Ms. Edwards?"

Oh good, we are back to last names, that only means one thing and it's not nice. Cameron is pissed.

"We didn't lose Charliee but yes, I can honestly say I can imagine some of what you are feeling..."

I am cut off when Cameron shoots up from his chair, looking down at me.

"You didn't lose both of your parents. Your friend is alive and home. Don't even attempt to tell me you have even the smallest idea of what we are going through."

His voice booms through the restaurant. I'm pretty sure we've caught the attention of everyone here. I try to understand his anger. Make an excuse for him yelling at me in front of everyone here, but no matter what I try to think about, I can't come up with enough of an excuse for him to make this big of a scene. He is right, I don't understand the loss the way he does. I do, however, understand the way the whole thing changed our lives.

I stand up and look right up at him. I'll be damned if I let people who are watching think he can yell at me and I'll just sit here and take it. We just stand, toe to toe, glaring at each other. Finally, I can't take it anymore.

"You know what, Mr. Tovaren? A lot of people's lives changed that day. Some more extreme than others. Some definitely lost more than others, but all of our lives changed if we had loved ones involved. I just wanted you to know if you needed someone who had some effect from the crazed man's action then I was here to listen."

I'm not going to stand here and have him embarrass me in front of everyone any longer. Walking past him, he stops me before I get too far.

"Where are you going?"

Really, he has to ask that question? Does he really think I would stay and be yelled at?

"Let go of my arm please, Mr. Tovaren."

"Ms. Edwards, you drove here with me."

Does he honestly think that is going to stop me from leaving? I would rather walk all the way home than be with him another minute.

"And I will be leaving on my own. Let me say this, though. If you get this mad with Jacob when he tries to talk to you, it's no wonder he is ignoring you."

Hurt fills his eyes and he quickly lets go of my arm. I feel bad for my words that I just threw at him. I know I'm hitting him where it hurts but I can't take them back now. When he looks away from me, I take that as my chance to walk away. Once outside, I pull my pone out and call Bryce. I'm not sure if this is a great idea since Bryce and his twin brother are cops.

These two are Charliee's brothers, which means I am like their little sister as well.

"Jayden, is Charliee all right?"

No hello first? I don't blame him. Both of the boys were there when they found Charliee and Levi, her hearing dog, buried under the building.

"Charliee is fine."

"Oh! Sorry, she told us you were going over tonight. We still kind of freak."

"Don't apologize, I understand. I'm actually not with Charliee right now. I had to change the plans, your mom is with her."

"What's up then?"

"Are you working right now?"

"We just pulled into the station and are heading home shortly."

"Would you mind taking a detour and picking me up and taking me home?"

"Not at all, are you all right? Where are you?"

I can hear the worry in his voice. I am getting ready to explain that I am all right, just out with a hotheaded jackass, but I hear Cameron coming up behind me calling out my name.

"Hold on, Bryce."

I place my phone on mute and then turn around. There is Cameron stalking toward me.

"How are you getting home?"

I hold my phone up. "I'm calling a friend to come and get me."

"I'll take you back to my place to get your car, Jayden."

We are back to first names. "I don't need you to take me

anywhere. Plus, you might not like something I say and push me out of the truck."

I swear I see a small smile.

"I wouldn't push you out of a moving car, Jayden."

I arch my brow at him.

"I would at least stop the car first."

I try not to smile, but I can't help it.

"Look, I'm sorry. I overreacted in there. If you would prefer someone to come pick you up and take you home, I understand."

After thinking about it for a moment, I take my phone off mute.

"Never mind, Bryce, I found a ride."

"Are you sure? I don't mind coming and picking you up."

My eyes never leave Cameron's. "I appreciate it, but I'm sure. The guy I'm with just apologized for being an ass, I've decided to give him another shot."

Cameron's eyes slant at me, but he is smiling.

"Jayden, if he is an ass, that won't change. I'll come pick you up."

I hear the concern in Bryce's voice, one of the reasons I love the boys. They would arrest anyone I asked them to without giving them a reason as to why.

"It was more of a misunderstanding."

"All right, but call me if things change. I'll come and get you and arrest him."

Like I said, they would arrest without question. Bryce confirming that makes me smile.

"Keep your phone close. I may take you up on that offer."

"Call or text when you get home, please."

"I will and thank you, Bryce. Bye."

Bryce says goodbye and then hangs up.

"Take him up on his offer?" Cameron's eyebrow shoots up in question.

Is Cameron jealous? I think about giving him something to think about but tonight has already been a whirlwind of emotions so it is better not to.

"Charliee has twin brothers who are cops. That was one of them, Bryce. He offered to come and pick me up and then arrest you."

I can't read his expression but I am pretty sure he is trying to figure out if I am joking or not.

"Protective brothers?" Cameron asks.

"You have no idea."

"I'm starting to get the idea." He takes a step closer.

I have to look up to look at him. I can feel the heat from his body, he is standing that close to me. My body craves to move closer to close the remaining little space between us.

"I will have to remember from now on that you have a lot of power in your hands."

I like this version of Cameron. It is fun and sexy. Although the other version is still in my mind. I know he is going through a lot right now, he has a very full plate, but there is no excuse for his little scene he created earlier. That is the one thing keeping me from reaching out to him right now.

"Don't you forget it!" I tease back.

He closes the space in between us, his arm going around my waist and pulling me into his body. I feel electricity shoot through all of my veins and straight to my core, but earlier is still nagging at me. Why can't I look at him like I usually look at a guy? Maybe a couple of fun dates and then move on, no strings attached. I don't know how to handle this other feeling. It is almost a need, a pull toward him. My mind is saying run from him and fast; my body is saying to tackle him and not let go.

He is going to kiss me again, I can read it all over his face. "Cameron, please don't."

He searches my eyes for a moment before he responds. "You want me to though. You want it as much as I do."

He has no idea how badly I want to kiss him right now. I still feel his lips on mine from the first time he kissed me, which is making asking him to back away all that much harder.

"I'm not going to stand here and lie to you, Cameron. Yes, there is a very large part of me screaming at myself to kiss you, but I'm going with the small part that is still pissed about the little scene you caused inside."

"So are you saying no to just kissing you tonight, or no to anything in the future?"

He is giving me that knowing, sexy smile he has. It is the same one he gave me that first day in the office when we met.

"It's a no, Cameron," I repeat, trying to sound convincing.

I need to step away. It is getting harder to ignore my need to kiss him with his body pressed against mine and that sexy smile looking down at me. My hands are on his chest and I find them gripping the front of his shirt tightly.

"Are you sure?" he asks as he looks down at my hands.

Absolutely not! That small part in my brain of reasoning is fading and almost gone. I release his shirt and push myself away from him. His arms fall to his sides and it takes everything I have not to throw myself back into his chest and take his lips myself.

Cameron watches me for a moment, like he is waiting for me to change my mind. The heat and need in his eyes has me mentally slapping myself for not giving in.

"All right, let's head out of here then." He turns and starts heading back to the truck. "I'll take you back to your car."

I don't say anything else, I just follow him to the truck. The ride back to his house is quiet. When we pull into the driveway, I quickly jump out, say goodbye as I close the door and quickly walk to my car. I need distance from him. I don't look back to see if he is watching me, I just leave as fast as I can. I'm not trusting myself to stay strong with my decision.

As I drive home, I try to figure out what I am going to do about this thing with Cameron. I need to figure this all out before I go back on Thursday for Jacob's tutoring. Maybe I won't have to worry about it. Maybe Cameron won't try anything else. I did just basically jump out of his truck before he came to a complete stop in the driveway, barely said a goodbye and left like I couldn't get away from him fast enough. He might take all of that as a hint that I'm not interested. Problem is, I am very interested, just not sure if I want to go further with all of this. We have chemistry, that is obvious, but the way he went off on me tonight kind of has me pushing away. He is broken right now, and not wanting any help. That alone should have me running, but if I have to be honest with myself, if I am running anywhere, I want it to be back against his chest and those lips!

It's been a week! Last Thursday when I went and tutored Jacob, Cameron was nowhere to be seen. I am pretty sure he was there, but the office door was closed and if he was in there then he made sure not to come out until I was gone. I found myself feeling disappointed as I said goodbye to Jacob and left. I wanted to charge into the office and make him talk to me, but what if he had someone in there with him, or he was on the phone with business?

I have done nothing but think about him and what happened last week during dinner. I think I'm using his outburst at the restaurant as an excuse to not get into anything with him. That is my way out. I'm not acting any better than Cameron was, only difference is he acted out in front of everyone, I am doing it all inside and blaming him for it all. I am driving myself crazy. Maybe I shouldn't fight this attraction we have and just see where it leads.

I need to remember Cameron is going through a lot right now. Any normal person would have mood swings and outbursts with everything he is going through. I've spent a lot of time with Charliee since she has been home. She is usually so happy and calm and even she has had an outburst of anger on a couple of occasions. Tragedy and loss can do that to a person. I don't get my feelings hurt with Charliee when she has her outbursts with me, why did I act so differently with Cameron?

Maybe I am overthinking all of this and reading too much into Cameron's actions. Sure, he has kissed me, and yes, he was going to kiss me the other night, but it doesn't mean we are in any kind of relationship. Wait! What the heck am I thinking about? Relationship? How did I go from nothing past a couple dates, no strings attached, to thinking the word relationship and Cameron in the same thought? I want to slap myself, again! Here I am, sitting in my car in front of Cameron's house, thinking about relationships. If Charliee was here right now she would fall out of the car in shock. I don't do relationships, why the hell am I thinking about it now? What has Cameron Tovaren done to me?

# CHAPTER NINE

Cameron

I saw Jayden pull up to the house. She has been sitting out there now for about ten minutes. Last week when she came by, I stayed in the office. I figured it would be best for both of us. When we got back from going out last week, she jumped out of the truck so fast, you would have thought she was scared to be alone with me any longer. I know my outburst was wrong at the restaurant, I have scolded myself over it many times. I finally just lashed out, and unfortunately it was at the wrong person. I knew it the moment she turned and walked away from me that night. I also know she wanted to kiss me just as much as I wanted to kiss her that night. The grip she had on the front of my shirt told me she wanted it, but she pushed herself away and I couldn't blame her.

When Jacob asked me today if he could go over to Tyler's

house, there was no way I was going to say no. It was the first time in almost a month that he even left the house without me making him get out. I knew today he had tutoring but I didn't care, I told him to go.

I was getting ready to text Jayden and let her know, but I decided not to. This would give me a chance to talk to her. Of course she needs to get out of her car first, and I'm not sure if she is going to. It looks like from here that she may be having a conversation with herself. She may be on the phone with someone, but I have a feeling she is talking to herself.

Another five minutes go by and finally her door opens and she steps out. I'm starting to feel a little guilty over the fact that I didn't call her and tell her Jacob wasn't going to be home. She might have had something else she needed to do. I am being selfish, but I need to talk to her and alone.

The doorbell rings. Well, let's see how much I can piss her off with all of this.

"Hi," she instantly says once I open the door. She looks surprised to see me.

"Hi, come on in." I move to the side and close the door behind her.

"Is Jacob ready?"

"Jacob isn't here."

She looks over her shoulder at me with a questioning look. "Is he going to be home soon?"

I just shake my head no.

She turns around to face me. That spark she gets in her eyes when she gets mad is there. "Did you not think of calling me and letting me know?"

I have to admit, I like it when she gets all fired up. Most women hide their feelings, but Jayden is definitely not like most women. I take a step closer; she doesn't move back, she holds her ground. I take another step, now close enough to wrap an arm around her waist and pull her body into mine. Her eyes never leave mine, but that anger spark she had earlier is now turning to fire and I am pretty sure she is no longer angry.

"Cameron, what are you doing?"

"Hoping you don't tell me no again."

She starts to say something, then stops. Once again, and then again nothing. The fire is still there in her eyes but there is something else now as well, almost a little fear.

"Jayden, what are you afraid of?"

Her hands are gripping my upper arms. "Cameron, I don't do the relationship thing."

"Relationship thing? Jayden, I think you are rushing this a little. I'm only asking to kiss you."

Her cheeks turn a little red from embarrassment, a look I never thought I would see on her. It is cute, then she looks away from me. This is all new domain for her, I have a feeling. I'm pretty sure she is used to being in control.

"So are you saying you aren't looking for a relationship?" she asks, looking up at me slightly.

I swear I see a little disappointment in her eyes this time. Why, I'm not sure, she is the one who just said she didn't do the relationship thing, which to be honest I am all right with. I don't usually do long-term either.

"No! What I'm saying is right now what I'm wanting is to kiss you."

Taking me completely by surprise, she grabs the back of my head and brings my lips down to hers, kissing me. I hear both of us moan a little. Her fingers are digging into the back of my head and she is up on her tippy toes trying to get closer to me. My arm that is around her waist tightens, my other hand I bury deep into her hair at the back of her neck. Our tongues find one another.

What the hell was I thinking when I decided to kiss this woman again? My body isn't satisfied with just her lips, I want more, I could even be all right with begging her for more. She has to be able to feel what she is doing to me. My arm is holding her tightly, our bodies are touching from chest to knees, and I know she feels how hard I am for her. What is it about this woman that is affecting me like this? I am ready, or actually fighting the need to pick her up and carry her up to my room. Maybe skip the walking up the stairs and just have her right on the stairs.

I take that back, I want her up in my bed all night long. My hand has the bottom of her shirt and when she moves slightly, my knuckles brush her skin. Just that slight touch and I am afraid I am going to explode right now. I feel like a teenager touching a girl for the first time.

"What are you doing to me?" I ask against her lips.

Jayden pulls back slightly, her eyes half-closed and looking dreamy. "I was wondering the same thing about you."

"Kissing you isn't going to be enough, Jayden. I thought it would be, but I was very wrong. I want you, all of you." There is that begging I was thinking about.

Again, she brings my lips to hers, the hunger she has very clear. I pull away. "Jayden, I wasn't joking. I want you and if you aren't wanting to do anything other than kiss then I can do that, but we will need to break for a few so I can calm my need for you down a little."

She gives me a small smile and before I can read what she is thinking, she pulls her shirt up and over her head.

"Does this work for an answer?"

"Are you sure?"

She nods. "Only thing I ask is it's not here in the living room. I don't want to risk Jacob walking in. Probably wouldn't be good for my job."

Grabbing her hand, I lead her up the stairs and to my room. I open the door and let her enter first. The moment I shut the door, she slams back into me, again bringing my lips down to hers. All she has on is her bra. Her skin is soft, I can't wait to feel her skin against mine.

I feel my shirt lift up my sides and my chest. She pulls back from me just enough to pull it over my head, and then her lips are back on mine. I unhook her bra and push the straps off her shoulders. Her bare breasts press against my bare chest and again, like the first time we kissed today, we both moan. How in the hell did I think I wasn't going to want all of her? She has all the control. She had it from the moment our lips touched and I am happy to let her keep it.

I feel her unbutton my jeans. I grab her around the waist and lift her up, carrying her to the bed. Sitting her down, I take a step back, I need to slow us down a little. Pulling off my boots and then stepping out of my jeans, I watch as her eyes look me up and down, her green eyes almost turning white. She lays back and stretches out over my bed, her hands going up over her head. She is giving me the control now. I don't mind, undressing her will be like unwrapping a much antici-pated gift.

As I slide her pants and remaining clothing down her legs, I find myself fighting the need to kiss every inch of skin as it becomes exposed, but I don't think I'll be able to control myself, I want in her that bad.

Jayden sits up after her clothes hit the ground. She smiles up at me and I wonder what is going through her mind, then her hand wraps around my hardness. Control is back with her. She looks up at me as she strokes me up and down, then up again. Her thumb circles the tip, smearing the beaded moisture around. I don't think I can get any harder, but I am wrong. I am going to lose myself right in her hand if she doesn't stop. I pull myself away from her touch and open the top drawer of my dresser. I pull the square package out and quickly place it on. Jayden has laid herself back down on my bed, watching me with hooded eyes.

"I need to be inside you now, Jayden."

She gives me the sexiest smile I have ever seen. "I need you inside me right now."

I watch as she spreads her legs, an invitation and the sign I need to tell me she is ready, and wanting just as I am. Grabbing her thighs, I pull her legs a little further apart and slide right between them. My tip is at her entrance. Just the slight feel of her wetness and the heat exploding from her body has me fighting to keep myself from exploding. I have to pull away from her slightly and take a few deep breaths. After a few moments, I push forward, burying myself further into her. I watch as Jayden's eyes close and her back arches up off the bed, thrusting her breasts up at me. An invitation I can't deny. I take one hard nipple into my mouth as I bury deep into her. She moans and her hands go to my backside, her nails digging into my cheeks as she tries to pull me even further into her. I gently bite the tip of her nipple, she gasps, and her back arches even more.

"You feel so good, Jayden."

She runs her nails up my back to my shoulders as her legs wrap tightly around my waist, holding me tightly inside of her.

"I need you to move, Cameron. Please!"

Hearing her beg is the sexiest thing I believe I've ever

heard. I've never been this turned on by a woman before. I know if I move, I won't last that long. I'm not ready for this to be over, to leave her body. I claim her lips once again. Her legs tighten around me, she is trying to thrust up. Now she's begging me with her body, and I can no longer hold back. I pull out almost all the way then thrust back into her hard and deep, she is tight. We both moan. Her wetness is gliding me easily in and out as I set a steady pace.

"That feels good, but I want you deeper." Her voice is quiet and a little rough.

I fell her tightening around me, she's close. I quicken my thrusts, doing everything to hold myself from my own release, but it's getting harder with each slide against her hot, wet, constricting walls. I pull out, my tip only enjoying the hot center of this woman, and with one last thrust into her my name fills the room and her body shatters around me, and I follow right behind her.

# CHAPTER TEN

Jayden

I wake up startled, forgetting where I am, and it's hot. I look around and remember that I'm in Cameron's room. We must have both fallen asleep. He is wrapped tightly around me, which would explain the heat. Looking out the window, I notice that it's dark outside. What time is it?

I turn my head and I'm able to see his face. Cameron always has a look on his face like he's thinking too much. Sleeping, he looks younger, more at peace, not like the world is falling apart around him. My heart breaks for him. I can't imagine what goes through his head these days with everything that has happened.

I try to listen and hear if Jacob is home. I don't want him knowing this happened, but I didn't plan on falling asleep and making this a sleepover either. I never stay the night with a guy, it seems too personal, too much like a relationship. I've never fallen asleep in a guy's bed after sex either, and here I am finding that not only did I easily fall asleep with Cameron, but I don't want to move right yet. I kind of like laying here. I like feeling his warmth against me, his arm around me. It's like I'm his and he isn't letting me go, protecting me even in his sleep. These are the feelings I have always tried to stay away from and here Cameron has created them inside of me with one night of sex.

Fear starts to spread in my chest. I swore I wouldn't feel this comfortable with a guy. I don't want to ever experience the pain my mom did when she found out about my dad cheating on her. I watched my mom go through a depression, even though she always tried to hide it from me, but I heard her cry herself to sleep every night. I used to go and sit outside her bedroom door and fight a need to go in and hug her. To tell her I was there, she wasn't alone, but she always worked so hard to put a strong face on around me. I didn't want her to feel worse that she wasn't fooling me. Sitting outside of her bedroom door kind of made me feel like I was there for her and still making her feel she was doing her best in front of me.

Looking over at Cameron once more, I make the decision. I need to walk away from him before I become too comfortable. Before I depend on him and these feelings he is beginning to create in me. Slowly I move out from under him, praying I don't wake him. This isn't an easy task when he is wrapped around me like he is afraid to let me go. It takes some time, but finally I am able to get up from the bed. He moves and I stand still, hoping that I didn't wake him. I watch as he settles himself onto his stomach, hugging the pillow under him. I take a deep breath and begin looking for my pants. Pulling them on, I take my phone out of the pocket, it is after eleven. I use the light to look for my shirt. I had it in my hand when we came in so I look by the door, finding it and pulling it on.

Cameron hasn't moved. I stand by the bed looking down at him. I am fighting the urge to climb back in bed with him. I quickly turn and leave the room before I find myself going against everything I have sworn against. As I turn to head down the stairs, a picture on the wall catches my attention. Well no, actually the dent in the wall next to the picture catches my attention first. It looks like someone punched the wall. The picture is of the Cameron, Jacob and their parents. It is easily ten years old. Jacob was so young, and Cameron's smile looks like he didn't have a care in the world. It is the perfect family. Both Mr. and Mrs. Tovaren were shining with pride. You can see it in their smile and eyes. They were proud of their family.

If I think back to the pictures of my family, my mom always had that smile and look in her eyes. My dad's smile never reached his eyes. It was always forced I realized as I grew up. It's funny what the mind thinks it sees until it's shown the truth.

When I reach the bottom of the stairs, the front door opens, Jacob is home. I see the surprise on his face. I'm sure I'm the last person he expected to walk in and see in his house this late at night. I'm sure you can see the embarrassment on my face. I got caught, by one of my students, leaving their house late at night, obviously from spending time with their older brother.

"It's late," Jacob signs.

I have nothing to say, I just nod my head.

"Why are you still here?"

He doesn't really need to ask that question, I'm sure.

"Are you tutoring my brother now?"

I am in too much shock to answer, but the booming voice behind me causes me to jump.

"Jacob!"

I turn to find a shirtless Cameron standing behind me about halfway down the stairs.

"You need to apologize to Ms. Edwards now," Cameron speaks and signs.

Both guys just stand there staring at each other, and here I stand right in the middle. A place I'm not comfortable in for more reasons than one.

"Is this the reason you were so happy that I wanted to go to Tyler's tonight, so you could do this?" Jacob signs to his brother and then points between Cameron and myself.

"I'm going to go, I'm sorry," I sign to Jacob, but speak as well so that Cameron can hear behind me.

Cameron comes down the couple of stairs and stops me before I can move. "You aren't leaving until my brother apologizes."

Cameron's eyes never leave his brother's as he speaks to me.

"Cameron, it's all right, really. I'm just going to leave," I try again.

I am surprised to see the anger forming in Jacob's eyes. I may only know him from school but I would have never thought I'd see that kind of reaction and anger out of him. He is always smiling and happy. The more I stand between the two men and watch them stare each other down, the more I am beginning to think Jacob's anger isn't because I am here with Cameron, but something between the two of them. I am just his excuse.

Cameron comes around so that he is facing me, his back to Jacob. "You don't need to leave, Jayden."

I look over his shoulder at Jacob, he is shooting daggers into his brother's back. This is definitely between them two, and they need to work it out. Cameron doesn't need an excuse to keep distance between them. We don't need to let this happen again, he needs to fix his relationship with his brother.

"This should never have happened, Cameron. Jacob's right in a way. I was here to do a job, not you."

Cameron flinches a little, almost like I slapped him. Shock shoots across his face, but only briefly, he recovers quickly. Now some of that anger is pointing at me. I can tell he is trying to read me. Good luck with that, Mr. Tovaren.

I expect him to try and stop me when I begin to push past him to leave, but he doesn't. I grab my bag from the floor by the stairs and quickly walk past Jacob. Stopping at the door, I want to turn and apologize. Tell Cameron it is everything opposite of a mistake, but then I think against it. I need to walk away from this, now before this becomes more to both of us. Opening the door, I almost run to my car. Slamming the door, I take a deep breath, my head going back to rest on the headrest. I know Cameron may never speak to me again. Isn't that what I want? My eyes burn a little. No, that isn't what I want. What the hell has Cameron done to me? I don't cry, especially over a guy!

I need Charliee, but it is midnight. Normally that wouldn't stop me but she is still healing and needs her rest. She probably wouldn't be a whole lot of help right now anyway. She keeps warning me that one day I am going to find a guy who is going to knock all my codes and rules for dating out the door. She would take much pride in telling me, "I told you so."

I need to go somewhere but I don't know where. I don't want to go home, it suddenly seems lonely. I run my hands over my face, looking around. I can't sit here in my car, in front of the Tovaren house. *Dammit, why didn't I just stay away?* I scold myself as I start my car. I have no idea where I am going but I'm not staying here!

---

It's been a crazy week. It started with Monday night with Cameron, to finding out Charliee was dating one of the hot firemen that found her that night of the bombing. I am happy for her, Travis seems like a good guy and he is very nice to look at. Charliee doesn't date much, I think she gets tired of guys treating her weird because she's deaf. She can't make it any easier for them, she talks and is usually pretty easy to under-stand. To top it off she reads lips like a champ, all you have to do is remember to look at her when you are talking. She has a great sense of humor when it comes to someone forgetting she's deaf, which is easily done since she talks so well. She caught me so many times when we first met.

Then Wednesday afternoon, Charliee stopped by the school and had lunch with me. She's been going crazy not being able to work. She told me about her date with Travis. I found myself becoming a little jealous. She was glowing and smiling from one ear to the other while she was telling me. Then she told me I needed a boyfriend. I almost told her about Cameron, but what exactly was I supposed to tell her? "Hey, I met Cameron Tovaren while I've been tutoring Jacob. One day he was not home so I ended up in Cameron's bed. We haven't spoken since." I could imagine the look she would give me.

I'm pretty sure she knows I'm holding something back from her. She gave me the questioning look when it all came up.

Cameron had text me this morning and told me there was no reason to come by for Jacob's tutoring, he wasn't going to be home. Nothing else was said. I thought about texting him back but what would I say? I know he was mad about the comment I made about us sleeping together not being a good idea, but honestly I just wanted out of that house and out from in between him and Jacob. I didn't tell him that the sex was amazing and waking up with him lying next to me was even better.

My phone ringing brings me out of my daze. Looking at the screen, my pulse quickens a little. Why is Charliee's brother, Derrick, calling me? Is something wrong with Charliee?

"Hello," I answer, my heart in my throat.

"Jayden, is Charliee with you?"

"No, I'm still at work, why? What's wrong?"

"There has been another explosion. This one was at the movie theater, no one can get a hold of her."

Normally I would put money on the fact that Charliee wouldn't be at the theater alone, but then again she has been pretty bored and going stir crazy lately so I wouldn't be surprised if she was. Plus, Travis could be off today and they could have gone. My veins go cold.

"I haven't seen or heard from her all day, but I'll text her and see if she responds to me."

"All right, please call me if you hear form her," Derrick's worried voice pleads with me.

"I will and please let me know if you find anything as well."

We both hang up and I immediately text Charliee.

**Where are you?

I wait what seems like forever for her to respond. I swear with each click of the clock in my classroom my heart beats faster. I am getting ready to text her again when I receive one from her.

**Give a person a chance to text back!! What is wrong with all of you??

I take a deep breath. She is all right. She sounds a little pissed, but she is safe.

I know she's feeling a little smothered right now. She has all of us surrounding her making sure she is safe, but she has no choice. She scared the hell out of us, we are keeping her close and she is going to have to get used to it.

I wait a little bit, I'm sure either her parents or her brothers are filling her in on what happened. After about ten minutes, I text her.

**Do you need me to come over tonight? I can stay with you.

She responds pretty fast.

**You have to work in the morning, I'm good. Actually I'd prefer a little alone time right now. I'll be all right. Love you.

Charliee usually doesn't like to be alone. She has always

liked having people around her. She doesn't go to restaurants alone, or the movies, or even shopping. Lately, though, I'm sure with all of us hovering over her, she may need some time alone. I don't want to leave her alone tonight, but I need to let her deal with this her own way.

**If you need me for any reason please text me, no matter what time it is. Love you too.

Again, she responds quickly.

**I will, I promise.

My thoughts then go to Cameron and Jacob. This news isn't going to be easy on them either. This lunatic is still loose and still trying to kill people. I want to call Cameron, but I am pretty sure I am the last person he wants to talk to right now.

My plan is to go home and soak in my hot tub. A glass of wine sounds amazing, but I don't want to drink anything that would keep me from driving to Charliee's if she needs me tonight. I'm not sure who is more surprised, myself when I find myself parked in Cameron's driveway, or Cameron when he opens the front door and finds me standing there.

"Hi." He doesn't invite me in, he just stands there in the doorway staring at me.

I don't like these feelings he is creating in me. He has me all twisted up and I'm not sure if I like it.

"I just heard about the bombing at the movie theater and wanted to come by and see how you guys were."

I sound pathetic to myself as I speak. Why would I need to come check on two grown men? Cameron's eyebrow arches a little, I think I surprised him.

"I was just watching about it on T.V. Jacob isn't here, he's at Tyler's house."

I watch as Cameron's muscles flex under his t-shirt when he brings his arm up to the door frame above his head. His shirt tightens across his chest. My hands itch to reach out and touch him and my body heats up with want. I need to leave before I do something to embarrass myself.

"Well, I'll see you later. I'm sorry if I interrupted anything."

I turn to leave, but only make it a couple steps before I decide I need to apologize for the other night. Turning, I find myself plastered against Cameron's chest. I hadn't even heard him move, and here he is standing right behind me. He isn't touching me, but I can feel the heat from his body. My hand comes up and rests on his chest. I can't stop them any longer, not being this close to him. I don't look up at him, though. I'm not sure if I want to see what his eyes may be saying.

"I'm sorry, Cameron," I speak into his chest.

He doesn't say anything back and he isn't touching me back. I am waiting for him to remove my hand and tell me to leave.

"What are you doing to me, Jayden?"

That brings my eyes up to his in surprise. Before I can say anything, his lips claim mine. His arms circle around my waist and pull my body up tight against his. I trail my hands up over his shoulders and to the back of his neck, one hand going into his hair. I hold onto him like a he is my lifesaver and he is keeping me from drowning.

Our lips separate and we just stand there, forehead to forehead. "Cameron, I'm sorry for what happened the other day."

He stands to his full height, pushing away from me a little. "Sorry for what part of the other day, Jayden?"

My mind can't think straight with our bodies touching. I take a step away from him, a chill running through my body with the heat of his missing. "I'm sorry for what I said the other day before I left. About us sleeping together being a mistake."

He takes a step toward me, but I take another one back. We need to have this conversation and I can't do that with him in touching distance, or I won't get anything out that I need to say.

"Wait, please," I hold my hand out in front of me to stop him from stepping closer to me once again. "I need to say this, Cameron."

He only nods and takes a step back, putting more space between us. Now that I have the space and all of his attention, I don't know what exactly it is that I want to say.

"Jayden, why don't we go inside and talk."

I'm not sure if being inside is a good idea. At least out here I will be able to control myself a little where he is concerned. Who the hell am I trying to kid? I lose all control with this man and forget where I am, inside or out won't make a difference I'm sure.

Nodding, I follow him inside, enjoying the view of his backside. *Stop!* I yell at myself.

"Would you like something to drink?"

*A beer, glass of wine, even a shot would be great,* I think to myself. "No, thank you."

He points over toward the couch. "Have a seat."

I sit and silently hope he will sit in the chair but no, he sits right next to me on the couch.

"So what do you want to talk about?"

How in the blue blazes am I supposed to think, let alone talk with him sitting so close to me? All I want to do is grab him and have a repeat of the other night.

I clear my throat and look down at my hands. "I just wanted to apologize for the way things ended the other night."

"That's what you said outside."

I take another deep breath, he isn't going to make this easy, is he?

"I should never have said what I did. I was embarrassed that Jacob caught me leaving. I don't blame him for being mad that night. I'm his teacher."

"Jayden, that is no excuse for the things he said to you. I understand he has anger in him right now, but that doesn't excuse him for being rude."

"Cameron, really, I understand..."

"No, I think part of the problem right now is that I'm creating excuses for his moods and attitude, but I think that may be the problem. I need to stop babying him. What he said was completely wrong."

"Cameron, have you tried to talk to Jacob?" I finally look up at Cameron and my heart breaks.

His eyes are downcast, he is rubbing his thighs, and he looks worried.

"One day I can't get him to leave the house or talk to any friends, the next I can't get him to stay home."

That brings another thing to mind that we need to talk about. Jacob missing all of his tutoring. Cameron is finally talking to me and I don't want to ruin that, but like he just said about Jacob, I can't keep backing down because I am afraid of how Cameron will react to the conversation. He needs to step up as well.

"That's another thing we need to talk about, Cameron.

Jacob hasn't been home for tutoring for a week, this can't keep happening or he is going to fall behind again. You might want to think about putting him back into school."

I watch as Cameron takes a deep breath, leaning back in the chair and running his hands through his hair. "There needs to be a manual on how to raise your teenage brother."

He is getting mad, it is written all over his face. "Raising kids in general doesn't look easy. I can't imagine taking over a teenage sibling after losing both my parents, Cameron. It's not going to be easy, but you can't give up on him either."

He sits back up, his elbows on his knees, his face in his hands. I place my hand on his knee. "Cameron, there are plenty of people willing to help if you just ask."

Still nothing but silence, he has shut down on me. "All right, well I'll be going. I'll be back on Monday for tutoring, please make sure Jacob is here. If you need to talk, Cameron, you know how to reach me."

I wait a second longer, hoping he will say something but no, he just sits there. I stand up, but Cameron moves quickly. Before I know it I am sitting on his lap, his arms tightly wrapped around me, his lips devouring mine. There is a plea behind the kiss. He is holding onto me like I will disappear if he lets go. It is creating all kinds of feelings through me. The feeling of being needed is pulling the strongest.

"Can I have you, Jayden, please?" he asks against my lips.

There is no way I can or want to tell him no. He needs me, and if I am going to be honest with myself, I need him.

"Not down here, Cameron. I don't want to risk Jacob and his friends walking in."

He doesn't even hesitate, he quickly stands up with me in his arms and I swear he runs up the stairs. He sits me down as he closes the door to his bedroom and I am pulling his shirt up over his head, trailing my hands down his shoulders and then over his chest, his stomach and then down to the button of his jeans. I unbutton them all the way down then bring my hands around, sinking them into the back of them, pushing his jeans and boxer briefs down over his waist, grabbing his very nice backside. My hands have itched to grab this man's cheeks since following him toward the house earlier.

His physical strength is obvious everywhere I touch. I don't think I've ever wanted to just stand in front of a man and just run my hands over his entire body, feeling the definition of his muscles.

"Jayden, I need to be inside of you."

His voice is husky in my ear. It sends chills down my very heated body. I step back and quickly remove my clothes, standing in front of him naked, open for him to take me anyway he wants.

He finishes removing his boots and pants. He closes the space between us, then pushes me back against the bedroom door. His lips travel all over my neck, then finally back to my lips. Every time he kisses me, I feel lightheaded. It feels like a quick shot of the best liquor going straight to my core, heating it up. Feeling his hardness between us just ignites that flame working at my core. Holding onto his shoulders, I begin climbing up his body. I feel like I can't get close enough to him.

One of his hands goes under my backside lifting me up, the other one guides himself as he enters me. The feeling of his full length gliding into me is intoxicating. His other hand comes around to my backside and he lifts me up, pulling himself slowly out as I push my hips down, thrusting him fully and deeply back in.

Our pace begins to speed up, my head falls back against

the door, which thrusts my hips forward and him deeper. His lips explore my breast. I am close, so very close, and then he stops.

"Jayden, I forgot protection."

My heart squeezes a little over the concern in his eyes. That is the moment it happens. Here I am pushed up against Cameron's bedroom door, my legs wrapped around his waist, him deep inside of me. I am doing something I swore I would never do—I am falling for a guy!

"I'm on the pill, Cameron. I'm clean, I've never had unprotected sex."

"I promise you, I'm clean."

My hands go from his shoulders to the back of his head, burying my fingers into his hair, bringing his lips back down to mine.

# CHAPTER ELEVEN

Cameron

"Cameron, it looks like we will be ready for final inspection on this track in about two weeks."

"Kevin, here is my problem. This track and the one down in Texas are going to be at the same time. So like I told Steve down there, as soon as you have a possible date, I need to know. The other one will have to be set around the first date set."

Silence stretches on the other end of the line. Kevin was my father's second in command up here in Washington. He has worked for our company as foreman for as long as I can remember.

"Cameron, how are you doing?"

The question catches me off guard for a moment but before I can answer him, Jacob comes into the room, signing to me that he is going to Tyler's. It is Monday, he has tutoring today, I sign for him to wait.

"Kevin, I have to go, Jacob just walked in and I need to talk with him. Please let me know of a date as soon as you can, please."

"All right!" You can hear the frustration in his voice that I didn't answer his question. "I'll call you when I have some more information. Cameron, if you need anything, please let know."

"Thanks, Kevin, I'll talk to you later."

After I end the call, I bring my attention back to my brother.

"You have tutoring tonight. You already missed last week," I sign.

Jacob shrugs his shoulders. "I've got it, I don't need it anymore."

"Maybe it's time we think about you going back to school."

"That would make you happy, wouldn't it?" he fires back at me.

Here we go again with the attitude. "Why would you say that? You go over to Tyler's every day now as soon as he gets out of school, maybe you need to be back in school. We agreed on a couple weeks."

"I'm not ready."

"Fine, then you need to continue with tutoring."

"For me or you?!"

I don't think I've ever wanted to punch my brother as much as I want to right now. "You're stepping on dangerous grounds. You have no reason to talk about Ms. Edwards like that."

We stare at each other for what seems like an hour. My brother stands almost at my height, we are eye to eye. Without saying another word, he turns and starts for the front door. I grab his arm before he makes it too far, turning him back to me.

"You aren't leaving today," I sign.

"You can't tell me what to do. You are just my brother, not my dad."

"What is wrong with you? Why are you mad at me?"

Emotions run through his eyes. One thing about the deaf, their faces and eyes are very expressive. He wants to say something, I can see him debating with himself.

The lights began to flash through the house and the doorbell sounds. "That will be Ms. Edwards."

Jacob doesn't make a move to answer it. I don't know what to do anymore. It takes everything I have in me not to throw my hands up and tell him to do whatever he wants to do. I walk over and open the door.

"Hi."

"Hello." She comes in past me and looks over at Jacob. "Hello, Jacob, are you ready?" she signs to him.

Jacob walks over to the two of us. "You can tutor Cameron today since that's what you would both prefer. I'm leaving."

Before I can respond, he runs out of the house and to his car.

"Jayden, I'm sorry. I don't know what's wrong with him.'"

"Cameron, he's hurting and right now he probably thinks I'm taking you away from him as well."

"How can you be taking me away from him? He hasn't said more than a dozen words to me since I've been home."

"You need to start putting your foot down, Cameron, you are letting him walk all over you."

"He is seventeen years old, Jayden. You don't put your foot down like he is five."

What did she want me to do, ground him? Like he said, I'm his brother, not his father.

"Cameron, he is still a kid who needs guidance. He is walking all over you and you are allowing him to. He needs parenting."

"Well, they're dead!" I shout.

Jayden flinches and takes a step back. Her shock quickly changes to anger.

"Then that means you need to step up, Cameron. You yelling and taking your anger out on me isn't going to work. I'm just trying to help."

"I don't recall asking for your help, Ms. Edwards."

"Really, Cameron, back to last names? Maybe you're right. If you are going to act like a teenager, how does anyone expect you to raise one?"

"Who the hell made you an expert? I don't think you have any right to tell me what and what not to do with Jacob. It is absolutely none of your business."

I know I am lashing out at the wrong person. I just can't seem to stop. She is here and I am pissed, she became the target, which isn't fair and I know it. I am getting ready to apologize but am stopped by the hellion in front of me.

"You, sir, are a jackass. Just because you are angry over the situation and frustrated, it doesn't mean you can turn it onto me. No need to worry about me interfering any longer, I'm done wasting my time with the two of you."

She turns and leaves me standing there staring after her. I know I should stop her, but I don't move, I just let her go. Maybe this is the best. I need to concentrate on the business, Jacob, and I still have all the legal affairs, I don't have time for more stress. Whatever we have is causing more problems between Jacob and I, and I definitely don't need all of that right now.

I do see the hurt in her eyes, behind all of the anger. My chest tightens, my anger completely disappears and I realize she is right. I am being an ass, she doesn't deserve that.

My phone rings back in the office. I pick it up and see Mr. Colter, Tyler's father's name up on the screen. My chest jumps, is something wrong with Jacob? I know he left here mad and was driving.

"Hello, Mr. Colter," I answer and hear the insecurity in my own voice.

"Hello, Cameron, please call me David."

"Is everything all right?"

"Jacob is here and safe. I'm sorry, I didn't mean to alarm you with my call."

I take a deep breath and try to calm my racing heart down.

"Cameron, if I'm stepping over lines with what I'm about to say, please feel free to tell me."

His timing couldn't be worse. I have a very strong feeling this is another person giving me their advice on what I need to do with Jacob. This is his best friend's father, though. I need to take a deep breath and listen.

"What's on your mind, sir?" I hope the edge isn't coming through my voice.

*Join the party*, I think to myself.

"At first Tyler would come home after coming by and would be concerned because Jacob wouldn't talk to him. Now he is here every day."

"I know, I'm sorry..."

"Cameron," David stops me, "we don't mind Jacob being here, he is always welcome. That came out wrong, I'm sorry. We are just catching small conversations, he is angry. Basically the reason I'm calling is I was wondering if you needed any help or advice. I know you're a grown man, but right now you have a lot to take care of. It's hard for parents to handle teenagers, let alone an older brother who has to take care of everything and a teenager because of the loss of their parents."

I don't know what to say. Part of me wants to yell some more and tell him I have everything under control. Another part of me wants to beg the man to tell me what to do about Jacob.

"Cameron, are you still there?"

I have a tight grip on my phone, my other hand fisted.

"Cameron?"

"Sorry, yes, I'm here. I appreciate your concern and your offer, sir. I think for now I've got it. Today I mentioned maybe it was time for Jacob to go back to school. He became mad, saying he wasn't ready."

I'm not going to add the part about Jayden.

"I agree with you, Cameron, I think it's time Jacob starts getting back to what he normally does. School I think is a good idea."

David is going to give me his advice it seems regardless of wanting it or not.

"He says he isn't ready yet."

"I know you just said you were good on handling everything, but I feel I need to give you a little advice, use it as you want. Jacob is going to test you. Do the opposite of what you say. Get mad, even yell and tell you he hates you. You need to remember to hold your ground. Don't give in to him all of the time because of what's happened, he will walk all over you if you keep giving into him."

Everyone today seems to have their opinion on what I need to do with Jacob. Jayden and now David Colter.

Someone is pushing me and wanting to see how far I can be pushed. I really don't need all of this right now. I already question myself on if I am doing anything right, all of this is almost showing me I'm not.

"David, I appreciate the call. I will keep all of what you said in mind."

"Just remember, we are here if you need anything."

"Thank you." I quickly end the call before I lose the last of my reserve and tell the man off. I am close to blowing up.

Sitting back in my father's chair, I look around. My eyes land on a picture of my mother my father had on his desk. She always knew how to handle us boys. We never questioned her. I think my brother and I were more afraid of what she would do if we screwed up than our father. She never raised her voice or a hand at us, but she had a look that we knew when we did wrong. I could almost see her giving it to me now. Disappointed in the way I am handling everything. I need to get out of this house. I have no idea where I think I need to go, but I can't be here.

Jayden

"This was a great idea, Jayden, my toes needed some attention."

All week I have done nothing but think of Cameron. Thursday I didn't even attempt to go by the house for Jacob's tutoring. I am done with all of that. As the weekend came around, I was finding it harder to not text Cameron. So instead I texted Charliee, asking if she wanted to hang out and go get pedicures.

"I'm just surprised you were able to pull yourself away

from your hunk of a boyfriend. I feel honored to have a little time with you," I tease her.

I have no room to talk, a certain good looking guy has been taking up a lot of my time until this week as well.

"I know and I'm sorry, but you can only blame yourself. You were the one always telling me I needed to find a guy," Charliee defends herself.

"Well, I'm rethinking it all now. I didn't realize it would take you away from me like this."

"Maybe it's time for you to find someone and we can double date."

Find someone? If only I knew if I had or not. Wait, what am I thinking? Cameron hasn't tried to get a hold of me since Monday night, I think it's safe to say I don't have a "someone". This is why I should stick with my rules of no relationships.

"All right, Jayden, what's going on? Are you seeing someone and not telling me about it?"

*No, I'm not seeing someone. I'm having sex with someone, but not seeing them*, I think to myself.

"Come on, Jayden. You followed me into the shower literally to get the story about Travis. Who is this guy you haven't told me about?"

Smiling, I think back to the day I found out she had gone to see the firefighter who pulled her out from the bombing. She had gone to the station and he asked her out the next day. I did follow her into the shower to get the details. She wasn't giving any information up and was trying to hide from me with taking a shower. That wasn't going to stop me from getting the details, I followed her in.

I shrug my shoulders. "There really isn't much to tell yet. I'm not sure if there is anything even starting. Honestly he infuriates me more than anything."

"So I'm guessing you like this guy?"

Like Cameron? Right now I'm not liking him very much. Maybe I just need to forget about him, and all of the great sex, and go back to my original dating rules. Or maybe just stay away from men altogether for a little while.

"I haven't said anything because I'm not sure if there is anything to tell." I can tell Charliee is trying to read me. It is hard keeping things from her. She can read me like no one else can.

"So what do you have planned after our toes?" This is why she is my best friend. She knows when to not push me. I know it is killing her to not know who it is, or what is going on, but she knows me well enough to know I am needing more time.

Today has been much needed time with Charliee. I even got her to go shopping after our toes and lunch, and she hates shopping. I had hoped to get Cameron off my mind, but now that I am home again, alone, all I can seem to think about is him. This is crazy. Why am I sitting around on a Saturday night, alone, thinking about someone who obviously doesn't think about or want me? When did I become one of those girls?

I should be out tonight, but Charliee didn't want to go out. She will probably spend the evening texting Travis at work. I have a very strong feeling my best friend is done with her going out days. I saw the look in her eyes today when we talked about Travis. She is in love. I can't blame her, Travis seems like a great guy. I think what convinced me about how much she means to him was today when she told me he was learning sign language. Charliee reads lips better than anyone. I only learned to sign after meeting her because I was fascinated with the language, not because we had a hard time communicating.

94

Travis is learning her world. There aren't many men out there like him. I'm glad Charliee found him. She, if anyone, deserves a guy like him.

Who am I kidding, I really have no want or desire to go out anywhere tonight either. What I want is to be with Cameron. Damnit, I'm one of those girls. I've actually fallen for a guy. Problem is, that guy doesn't want me.

# CHAPTER TWELVE

Jayden

"This was a great idea, Jayden, my toes needed some attention."

All week I have done nothing but think of Cameron. Thursday I didn't even attempt to go by the house for Jacob's tutoring. I am done with all of that. As the weekend came around, I was finding it harder to not text Cameron. So instead I texted Charliee, asking if she wanted to hang out and go get pedicures.

"I'm just surprised you were able to pull yourself away from your hunk of a boyfriend. I feel honored to have a little time with you," I tease her.

I have no room to talk, a certain good looking guy has been taking up a lot of my time until this week as well.

"I know and I'm sorry, but you can only blame yourself. You were the one always telling me I needed to find a guy," Charliee defends herself.

"Well, I'm rethinking it all now. I didn't realize it would take you away from me like this."

"Maybe it's time for you to find someone and we can double date."

Find someone? If only I knew if I had or not. Wait, what am I thinking? Cameron hasn't tried to get a hold of me since Monday night, I think it's safe to say I don't have a "someone". This is why I should stick with my rules of no relationships.

"All right, Jayden, what's going on? Are you seeing someone and not telling me about it?"

*No, I'm not seeing someone. I'm having sex with someone, but not seeing them,* I think to myself.

"Come on, Jayden. You followed me into the shower literally to get the story about Travis. Who is this guy you haven't told me about?"

Smiling, I think back to the day I found out she had gone to see the firefighter who pulled her out from the bombing. She had gone to the station and he asked her out the next day. I did follow her into the shower to get the details. She wasn't giving any information up and was trying to hide from me with taking a shower. That wasn't going to stop me from getting the details, I followed her in.

I shrug my shoulders. "There really isn't much to tell yet. I'm not sure if there is anything even starting. Honestly he infuriates me more than anything."

"So I'm guessing you like this guy?"

Like Cameron? Right now I'm not liking him very much. Maybe I just need to forget about him, and all of the great sex, and go back to my original dating rules. Or maybe just stay away from men altogether for a little while.

"I haven't said anything because I'm not sure if there is anything to tell." I can tell Charliee is trying to read me. It is hard keeping things from her. She can read me like no one else can.

"So what do you have planned after our toes?" This is why she is my best friend. She knows when to not push me. I know it is killing her to not know who it is, or what is going on, but she knows me well enough to know I am needing more time.

Today has been much needed time with Charliee. I even got her to go shopping after our toes and lunch, and she hates shopping. I had hoped to get Cameron off my mind, but now that I am home again, alone, all I can seem to think about is him. This is crazy. Why am I sitting around on a Saturday night, alone, thinking about someone who obviously doesn't think about or want me? When did I become one of those girls?

I should be out tonight, but Charliee didn't want to go out. She will probably spend the evening texting Travis at work. I have a very strong feeling my best friend is done with her going out days. I saw the look in her eyes today when we talked about Travis. She is in love. I can't blame her, Travis seems like a great guy. I think what convinced me about how much she means to him was today when she told me he was learning sign language. Charliee reads lips better than anyone. I only learned to sign after meeting her because I was fascinated with the language, not because we had a hard time communicating.

Travis is learning her world. There aren't many men out there like him. I'm glad Charliee found him. She, if anyone, deserves a guy like him.

Who am I kidding, I really have no want or desire to go out anywhere tonight either. What I want is to be with Cameron. Damnit, I'm one of those girls. I've actually fallen for a guy. Problem is, that guy doesn't want me.

# CHAPTER THIRTEEN

Cameron

This last past week has been hell. First the incident with Jayden. Wednesday, Steve called and informed me we once again had vandalism on the track. This time, though, the group was caught. So hopefully this will be the last time. Unfortunately, the damage is large and will be expensive to repair. Not one that would set final inspection back, which, right now, I don't need. The two tracks are already too close together with dates only a couple weeks apart, the Texas site finishing first. Now they are closer.

Yesterday, Kevin called and one of our workers who was working on the roof fell and had to be taken to the hospital. He dislocated his knee and had some stitches on his forehead. To top everything off, this morning I told Jacob he was going back to school on Monday. He didn't respond at all, but that saying "if looks could kill," yep, I would have been shoved six feet down. He just walked up to his room and I haven't seen him since.

I've had about two hours of sleep each night. Every time I lay in my bed and shut my eyes, I see Jayden spread out on my bed, naked, begging me with her eyes and parted legs to take her. I have no idea how many times I've started to call and text her, apologizing for everything that happened Monday, but never did.

Maybe it is a good thing to keep things this way. Do I really need any more obstacles in my life right now?

Jacob's door slams upstairs, now is the time to prepare for the next round of fun. Last night after he went to bed, I went up and took his car keys. I am done with this anger shit he has been dealing out to me. He isn't leaving to go to Tyler's again until we talk.

"My keys?" Jacob signs the second he comes off the stairs.

I don't respond. Strange, earlier when I thought about all of this, I had plenty to say. Now, I can't figure out where to start.

"Where are my keys?" he asks again.

"I have them."

"You had no right to come in my room and take them."

"We need to talk."

"I have nothing to say."

"Jacob, you need to tell me why, since I've been home, you've acted like you don't want me here."

Instead of answering, he begins to look around. I pull the keys out of my pocket and hold them up until he notices them.

"You want them, then talk. What have I done that has pissed you off so much? I know it's not the whole Ms. Edwards thing, you weren't talking to me before that."

He stands there glaring at me. Tears are in his eyes, which almost causes me to lose it altogether. He is fighting something.

"Jacob, talk to me."

"You weren't here!" He signs it with so much anger, I almost feel like each word punches me in the chest. I wasn't here? What is he saying?

"Wasn't here for what?" I sign back.

Complete silence fills the room. He isn't answering me.

"Jacob, what wasn't I here for?" I try again.

"When they died." His motions are flat and tears fall from his eyes.

I feel like someone has their hands around my throat and bricks are sitting on my chest. Is he blaming me for our parents dying?

"How would I have stopped that?"

"You can go back to Texas." He grabs for his keys but I pull them back. Then it clicks.

"Jacob, I got here as fast as I could. I'm sorry I wasn't here when you found out."

When I moved to Texas a few years ago, Jacob said he was going with me. Of course, our parents would never have let that happen. I knew he wasn't happy I moved away, but I would have never guessed in the time I was gone, he was mad at me for going. We texted every day. We did talk about him coming down after graduation next year, but he never gave me any clue he was that mad that I moved away.

"Why do you think I'm going back to Texas?" Does he honestly think I am going back to Texas and leaving him here?

"None of your stuff is here," he signs.

No, it isn't. I haven't brought my stuff up. I knew I had to go to Texas for the final inspection of the track. At that time, I was going to talk to Steve about becoming one of my partners and taking over the Texas side of our business. I was going to fly down and then drive my stuff back. Did Jacob honestly think I was going to leave him here?

Jacob reaches across, catching me off guard, and grabs his keys out of my hand. Before I can stop him, he is out the door.

Shock is the best word I can think of to describe how I feel right now. That's what this has been all about. He thinks I am going to leave him here and go back to Texas. I know he's seventeen and all. I know the school has boarding, but never did it even cross my mind to leave him here alone. I knew from the moment I got the call from David Colter that my parents were killed in the bombing that I'd be moving back here to Washington. To be honest, I don't know if even my brother had been well into his twenties when all this had happened, I would have gone back. I have even already gotten a hold of a realtor in Texas to start putting things together to put my house up for sale.

Before I can even stop myself, I grab my phone and find Jayden's name and send her a text.

**I need you at my house.

I hit send. I need someone to talk to and Jayden is the only one I can think of to talk to about all of this.

# CHAPTER FOURTEEN

Jayden

When I received the text, I had to look twice at who it was from.

** I need you at my house

Did Cameron text it to the wrong person? I read the text over and over, like somehow it will change. Why does he need me at his house? It is probably a mistake, he probably meant this for another girl. I could text back and let him know, wrong person buddy, but if he texts back sorry, well then...

Wait, what if something is wrong? That must be it, something is wrong. I quickly grab my keys and wallet, running out to my car.

I think I run two red lights, but I make it to the Tovaren

house probably in record time. Running up to the front door, I ring the doorbell. My imagination is going crazy. I almost just walk straight in. I swear if someone doesn't answer it soon, I am going to just walk in.

I go to grab for the knob when the door finally opens, and there stands Cameron.

"What..."

Cameron grabs me, pulling me up tight against his chest, his lips taking mine. My body instantly melts. Just this man's lips can cause me to turn to mush.

Finally, my brain turns back on. What the hell is going on? Ending the kiss and taking a step back is one of the hardest things I've done. My body wants to go back, but my brain needs answers.

"Cameron, what's going on?"

He reaches out for me, but I take another step back.

"Again, let me ask, what's going on? Is Jacob all right? Are you all right?"

"Physically, everyone is fine," he finally speaks.

Unbelievable, what is he playing at?

"Seriously, that's your answer?"

Passionate heat is turning to angry heat. Who the hell does he think he is? After the way he yelled at me, he thinks now he can just text and I'll come running? To top it off, he thinks he can just pull me against him and kiss me? Wait! That is exactly what just happened. I came running with a text. Fool me once, my bad, but not anymore.

Shaking my head, I turn to leave. "Jayden, wait, please."

Something in his voice doesn't sound right. His plea stops me, something is wrong.

"Listen, can we just go inside and talk, please?"

Do I really want to go back to this? Sure, earlier I was

sitting at home missing him. Now I am still a little pissed that he thought I would just come over and act like nothing happened.

"Jayden, look, I'm sorry. I had no right to take my anger out on you the other day. I have no good excuse. All I can say is sorry."

His eyes are pleading with me. Why can't I stay mad at this guy? I'm not going to make it easy on him though. I will listen, I can't walk away from those eyes. Not saying anything, I walk past him and into the house. I sit down in the chair, this will be safer than sitting next to him on the couch.

"Thank you," Cameron says, sitting down on the couch.

"What did you need to talk to me about?"

"Today, Jacob and I had a little talk. Well, actually I think I did most of the talking. Anyway, I believe I figured out why Jacob isn't talking to me. I'm still a little confused about all of it, but it's nice to have some reason."

I am trying to be patient and listen to where he is going with what he is talking about, but I am running pretty short on patience right now.

"Cameron, what's happening?"

"Jacob is mad at me because I live in Texas."

Live in Texas? Why would Jacob be mad at him for that right now?

"I don't understand."

"Neither did I at first. Today I finally asked him what I did that has made him so angry with me, besides sleeping with you."

I know I blush a little, my face instantly becomes warm. "So you think he is mad because you moved?"

Cameron nods. "When I moved away, he said he was going with me, but of course we all knew that wasn't happening. Anyway, I believe he thinks I'm leaving again and without him."

"You haven't talked to him about any of this before now? Honestly, why wouldn't he think you would be going back? If I thought about it, I would have thought the same thing."

Another reason why getting involved with Cameron probably isn't a good idea. How long can he stay? His home and business are down in Texas.

"No, honestly I haven't really thought about the need to talk to him about it. He hasn't said much to me since being home. I told you that night we went out for drinks he wasn't talking to me. Then he only became more distant after finding out about you and me. Plus, he is a kid, why would I talk to him about my personal life?"

Personal life? Men! I would have thought Cameron and Jacob would have talked about what's happening next. Jacob is probably too worried to ask. Of course he would be worried about what was going to happen to him next. If Cameron was going to push him off to another family member or what.

"Cameron, he probably thinks you are going to leave him again. Then again, why wouldn't he think that if you haven't talked to him about any of the plans? What are you planning on doing?"

"Even if I was going back to Texas, I would have taken him with me, I wouldn't leave him here alone. I decided to move back here anyway. He only has one more year of high school left, I wouldn't take him away from his friends on his senior year."

"Have you told him that now that you have figured out what's wrong with him?"

"No, he never let me explain anything. He took off to Tyler's again. He told me that since I haven't brought my stuff here, my truck and house things, he figured I'd be going back. He is also mad that I wasn't here when everything happened."

Everything happened? Cameron can't even say what happened. His parent's died, by the hand of a very selfish human being, and he can't say it. That can't be good for any of their anger, they both need to talk about it.

"Cameron, you couldn't have stopped the bomb from going off, or your parent's going out to dinner."

"I know that, and Jacob isn't thinking I could. He was with Tyler's family when he found out. I'm thankful for that, but I wasn't here until the next day. I took the first flight I could get, but it took some time for me to get here."

"So what you are saying is that you believe Jacob's been mad at you for leaving in the first place, this just created enough to bring that anger out. Were you two always real close?"

Cameron laughs a little. "No, actually when he was born I was pissed at my parents for having another kid. I was eleven and didn't like that I wasn't getting all the attention any longer. When he was about five, we were at a restaurant and some kids were making fun of him because he was making sounds instead of talking. I got pissed at the kids, but when the father started laughing I got up, walked past him and kicked his chair out from under him. From that moment on, I swore no one would pick on him again and we were always together from that point on. My friends learned that if I was going to be around, so was my brother. He never left my side unless we were in school."

"How mad was he when you moved away? That must have been hard on him."

"He was upset, but we have texted each other every day I've been gone. I always told him he had to finish school and then afterwards he could come down to Texas. He had texted me a couple times the day everything happened. I was dealing with problems with work and had forgotten to read the text and answer him. Finally, Tyler's dad got a hold of me later that night and told me what had happened."

I want to talk to him about talking about what happened with his parents and their death. On the other side of it, I don't want to be yelled at again for telling him what to do. So I decide to let it go for now.

"So you didn't tell him you weren't going back to Texas?"

"He didn't give me a chance. I was a little shocked and before I could explain what my plans were, he ran out. I have to go to Texas for final inspection in a couple weeks and planned on bringing all my stuff back then."

I don't know what I should or shouldn't say. Every time we discuss Jacob and I voice my opinion or a suggestion, Cameron ends up telling me to mind my own business and yells at me. Now he is staring at me like he is expecting me to tell him what to do.

"Cameron, every time I say something, we end up in a fight. Please don't look at me like you are waiting for me to give you a suggestion on how to handle this."

"Jayden, I said I was sorry."

Does he really think that is all it is going to take?

"Cameron, you haven't only yelled at me once, but twice. Once in public. You apologized after that time as well, but that didn't stop this last round we had."

He looks down at his hands. Nothing is said for a good amount of time. I am about to say that I am just going to leave when he finally speaks.

"I needed someone to talk to. You are the only adult I have spoken to since being home. Even Tyler's dad called and tried giving me some parenting advice. I already know I'm not doing a great job with Jacob, everyone telling me what I should be doing is only confirming that. I'm not sure what to do with Jacob. This isn't the kid I know. I'm used to the happy kid he has always been."

Hearing the pain in Cameron's voice makes me want to go over and hold him. I know he basically just told me he wants my advice, but I still feel like I am going to have to watch what I say. He came to me when he needed someone to talk to. My chest expanded some when he said that. I don't trust myself to be sitting next to him but I need to touch him.

Reaching over, I place my hand over his. "Cameron, I wasn't trying tell you that you weren't doing things right with Jacob the other day and I'm sure Mr. Colter wasn't meaning for you to feel that way either. Your world has been flipped upside down. Losing both of your parents, having to care for your brother, run your family's company and somewhere in there, you need time to grieve. I'm pretty sure you haven't done any grieving. I know I was only trying to help and I'm pretty sure Mr. Colter meant no different. Jacob is a great kid. You are right, he was always happy. Smiling all of the time. He was always in a large group of people. You have to remember his world was turned upside down as well. Like you getting mad at me because you had no one else to get mad at, he is mad as well, and you are the one who he is going to aim his anger at."

Holding my breath, I wait for him to say something, hoping I haven't stepped over a line. His hand just holds mine tightly. His voice is low when he finally speaks. So low I almost don't hear him.

"I miss them so much," he whispers, and it tears my chest wide open hearing the pain in his voice.

I can't stay away from him any longer. Kneeling down in front of him, I place my hand on his cheek, trying to get him to look at me. I feel the wetness, knowing he is crying shatters me. This strong, hard-faced man is crying. I feel the tears well up in my eyes. He doesn't move, he just keeps his head hanging down.

"Cameron, look at me."

Nothing, he almost seems distant. Since my hand is still on his cheek, I push his face up. His eyes look anywhere but at me. Almost like he is embarrassed to show me his pain.

"You should never be ashamed of showing your pain, Cameron. You're not a robot. No one expects you to be strong all the time. Asking for help isn't a bad thing. Showing that your parents' death is affecting you isn't something to be ashamed of."

His eyes finally look at me. The tears are gone, but I can still see the hurt in them. A man who just lost both of his parents that he loved very much. If I wasn't hooked completely on this man before, I am now.

Slowly, he brings his head down to rest his forehead against mine. He is wanting to kiss me. He wants to know if I have forgiven him yet. I circle my hand around to the back of his head, digging my fingers into his hair and bringing his lips down to mine.

Our lips touch and for the first time, it isn't raw. His lips are smooth and tender. He isn't crushing our lips together, eagerly seeking out my tongue with his. Instead, he moves them lightly against mine. There is a tender side to this man and my heart flips in my chest for him. I have officially fallen for a guy!

"Jayden, I have never known a woman like you before."

His voice is husky. I'm not even wondering if what he said

is a good or bad thing. Everything right now is good. The feelings racing through my body, the way my heart trips every time his lips tenderly touch mine, everything is good.

"You are one of a kind as well."

"I want to take you upstairs now."

"Are you asking me if I forgive you?" I smile against his lips.

"I'm really hoping you forgive me. I hear make up sex is the best kind of sex."

I think I like playful Cameron. "Is that all you want me around for, my body?"

His smile fades. "Is that what you think?"

I don't want the playful Cameron to leave. I bring my hands down to the top of his jeans, unbuttoning the fly of his pants. I run my hands up and under his shirt, running them up his stomach to his chest.

"I'm using you for your body!" I smile up at him, looking through my lashes.

His smile returns. Or maybe it is more like a cocky grin. Before I can guess what he is going to do, he is up on his feet with me slung over his shoulder and heading up the stairs.

"This is so caveman," I say as my hands smack his backside.

"I could drag you up the stairs by your hair, woman."

"Hair pulling sounds fun, just in bed though, not being dragged by it up the stairs."

We reach his room. Cameron sits me down and starts working out of his clothes. I quickly discard my own. We are standing in front of each other naked in no time. He takes a step closer to me, our bodies barely touching. His arm goes around behind me. I feel him grab my hair and twist it around his hand. He pulls down, forcing my head back, his lips instantly going to my neck.

"I like your hair, Jayden," he whispers.

Electricity shoots through my body. He pulls a little harder and I moan. I feel him smile against my neck.

"You like it a little rough, do you?"

He starts walking me backwards toward the bed. The back of my legs hit the softness of the mattress. Without releasing my hair, he turns me around, now my back is against his chest. His other hand starts at my thigh and slowly runs up my leg, over my hip, to my back. Once his hand makes it to my shoulder, he gently pushes me forward, my chest now against the bed. I can feel his hardness against my backside. Cameron's hand comes back down my back, once he comes to my hips his hands come around to my front and two fingers slide deep inside of me.

"You're so wet, Jayden. So ready for me."

"Cameron, please," I beg and push my backside against his hardness.

He removes his fingers, I moan again. At once he pulls my hair again and enters me with one quick thrust. I bite my lip to keep from yelling. I feel him slide out almost all the way and then once again thrust into me, again pulling my hair. The sensation is like nothing I've ever felt before. The pleasure of him filling me so completely and deep, with the sting of my scalp from where he pulls my hair. It takes no time at all to lose myself. My insides tighten around Cameron's hardness, my body begging him to release with me.

# CHAPTER FIFTEEN

Cameron

This woman is capturing my heart. I never thought that would happen. I was always too busy with work to open enough time in my life for a relationship. Or maybe I just never found someone who made me want to create extra time for them. Now here when timing is crazy with both sides of the business to run, dealing with Jacob and still finishing up with business from my parents' deaths, Jayden appears in my life.

Jayden is still asleep, her head resting on my chest, her leg slung over mine. She had said she didn't do the relationship thing as well. Now I wonder what she meant by that.

Hearing the door shut downstairs, I figure Jacob just got home. Looking over at the clock, I'm shocked that it is only seven, he's home early tonight. I hate to wake Jayden, she is sleeping pretty sound, but Jacob and I need to talk. I need to clear things up with him, we can't keep going the way it has been. I try as soft as possible to move out from under Jayden, even though my body right now only wants to stay where I am. She can stay up here and sleep while I go and talk to Jacob, we aren't going to hide whatever this is between us.

Once I move away, Jayden stirs and quickly settles back to sleep. Throwing my jeans back on, I grab my shirt and leave her sleeping there in my bed.

I find Jacob in the kitchen, looking through the fridge. I lean against one of the counters and wait for him to turn around. A few moments pass and finally I have his attention. I wait for him to roll his eyes and try to jet past me but instead he surprises the hell out of me and matches my stance against an opposite counter.

"You are home early," I sign after a few moments of both of us just standing there staring at each other.

He only nods his head.

"Jacob, we need to talk and clear a few things up."

Again, he only nods with agreement. It seems like I'm going to be the one doing all the talking, which is fine, he needs to know what I have to say.

"Let's start with the school issue. I called the principal yesterday and told him you would be back on Monday. I think it's time to start getting back to life."

Jacob stares down at the coke can he is drinking out of. After a minute, he sets it down on the counter and then finally looks back up at me.

"I'm not sure what exactly a regular life is anymore, but I will go back on Monday."

A little shocked, all I can do is stare at him in surprise. He has gone from a very angry, almost childlike temper tantrum earlier today to my seventeen-year-old, mature brother. What happened in between to change him that fast?

"Jacob, we are going to have to adjust to a new life, both of us. Mom and Dad are gone, we will have some changes, which brings me to the next thing. I don't know why you thought I would leave you here alone and go back to Texas, but I never even thought that. In a couple weeks, I will have to go to Texas and go through the final inspection on the track home down there but afterwards, I'm packing everything and coming home here. I have already looked into selling my house there, it's on the market already."

"What about the business down there in Texas, how are you going to run that from here?"

"I can do most of the work from here, paperwork wise. I may have to make a trip down there every once in a while but Steve will actually run the projects."

"Tyler's dad told me today that I needed to talk to you."

So that's what changed in the last couple of hours. It pisses me off a little that Jacob will listen to Mr. Colter, but wouldn't give me a chance to talk to him. I instantly cool my temper, at least someone was able to get through to him, now maybe we can start fixing things from this point on.

Jacob looks down at my bare feet, "I saw Ms. Edwards' car outside."

It isn't a question. I just nod, now we need to figure out this problem. Get everything out in the open and start fresh.

"I'm not sure how I feel about you sleeping with my teacher."

I understand his feelings, if I am honest with myself I'm not sure how I feel about sleeping with his teacher. Obviously not for the same reasons as his, but all the same.

"I'm not just sleeping with her, I think I'm starting to like her more than that," I confess to him.

As he stares at me, you can see him thinking about it.

"Just don't push it on me."

Push it on him? I haven't pushed anything on him, especially Jayden and me. I'm not going to tip-toe around him, though, he needs to know she is going to be around.

"Look, first off you need to apologize for the things you have said to and about her. You were completely out of line to attack her like that. Second, I'm not going to push you to like the situation, but I am letting you know now that I'm not ending anything with her. She will be around and you need to get used to it."

He doesn't say anything else, he just nods. Pushing off the counter, I walk over to him. "Jacob, you're my little brother, I will always be here for you, even when we grow old and have lives of our own."

For the first time in a long time, Jacob smiles. "When we grow old? You are already old."

"Not too old to kick your butt still." Laughing, I hug him. This is my brother, I'm glad to have him back

"You could try, old man, you could try," he signs as he walks past me and out of the kitchen.


Quietly opening my bedroom door, I find Jayden fully dressed and sitting on the edge of the bed.

"Everything all right?" she asks.

Walking over to her, I grab her hand and pull her up onto her feet, claiming her lips.

"I'll take that as everything went well," she answers her own question, a little breathless.

117

"I guess Mr. Colter had a little talk with him and convinced him to finally talk and listen to me."

"How do you feel about that?"

"At first it pissed me off. After thinking about for a minute, I realized as long as it got us talking, why do I care if it took someone else to get through to him as long as someone finally did?"

"So everything is good now?" Her eyebrow rises up in question.

She isn't talking about between Jacob and me, she is talking about how Jacob feels about her being here with me.

"I'm sure we will have some bumps here and there, I'm not expecting everything to go perfect, but I think it will definitely be better between us now."

She doesn't say anything. She just looks up like she is waiting for me to continue. She wants to know about how he feels about us.

"He knows he owes you an apology."

"Cameron, don't force him on that. I understand his reaction."

"Jayden, for one he was raised better than he treated you. Second, he had no right to say the things he did. He should be respectful, and he was anything but that."

"A lot has happened, Cameron. He was going through an anger stage."

"Jayden, don't make excuses for him being rude. He needs to apologize."

She wants to continue arguing with me, I can see it in her eyes, but what he did there was no good reason to excuse. He should never have said what he did, regardless of how he felt about the two of us being together.

"So he's all right with this?" She gestures with her hand between the two of us.

"What are we saying this is?" I mimic her gesture between the two of us. "Jayden, you are the one who said you don't do the relationship thing."

Shrugging, she looks down. "I've never done the relationship thing, Cameron."

Well that is a surprise to hear. "Was that a choice of yours?"

I have a hard time believing she has never been in a solid relationship due to no interest. I have a feeling it has to be a choice she has made, but why? I watch as she sits down on the edge of the bed, her hands between her thighs, eyes looking down.

"It's a long story, but I'll give you the short version." She looks up at me, "I thought my parents had a perfect marriage. A couple completely in love. One day I came home from school to my mom bawling in the kitchen. She had been completely in love with my father. My father, however, was sleeping with others. I watched my mom almost completely fall apart from a broken heart. I never wanted to feel that broken. I decided as long as I didn't let anyone in, then they couldn't break me when they decided they wanted out."

"You haven't been in a relationship because you think whoever you decide to be in a relationship with will cheat on you?" I don't even try to hide my surprise. Jayden seems like too strong of a person to allow someone to break her.

"Cameron, I watched my mom hurt and go through hell because of how much she loved my father and he didn't return the same love to her. She tried to act strong around me, but at night I would hear her crying, alone in her room. I would sit outside her door and listen to her. My dad did that to her."

"Jayden, not everyone cheats. How is your mom now?"

"Great! She is remarried to a great guy that she met here in Washington. I grew up in Tennessee, but once everything happened, Mom and I moved here. My mom has family here."

"So your mom remarried and is happy. That should prove to you that there is love in a relationship. Not everyone is like your dad."

She doesn't say anymore. She just sits there playing with her nails. Kneeling down, I grab her hand. She looks me in the eyes, I see the fear, and it tears at my chest. This strong woman is showing fear, showing me her weakness.

"What is this we have going on here, Jayden?"

"Cameron, earlier today before you sent me the text, I was sitting at home, thinking about you. I was having very mixed feelings. I haven't stopped thinking about you since we met. From the moment I walked into Mr. Lennerd's office, you have had an effect on me. Then you basically told me to step away. No one has affected me the way you have, and honestly it scares the hell out of me."

"Jayden, I can't tell you what the future will hold. I have definitely learned that life can change in a second. One thing I can say is I'll never cheat. One woman at a time is all I want or can handle."

Laughing, she smacks me on the arm. "We aren't that bad. Trust me, you guys aren't as easy as you think you are. You said yourself you don't really do the relationship thing either. Why has that changed?"

"Because a few weeks ago, this fireball fell into an office I was at for a meeting and I haven't been able to think straight since."

I wait as she searches my face. She is thinking, you can see the wheels turning behind her eyes. She leans forward, I think she is going to kiss me but she stops close enough that I can feel her lips against mine when she speaks. "All right, let's try this relationship thing."

I gave her a light kiss. "I'm not going to promise I'll be easy to deal with, I'm kind of cranky."

"Kind of cranky?! That's putting it nicely."

Moving quickly, I stand back up but push her back so that she is laying on the bed, leaning over her. "Does this seem cranky to you?"

She laughs, pushing against my chest. "As much as I'd like to see this cranky side, I'm starving, for food. Some cranky guy has been playing with my head, which has played with my appetite."

Pushing up off the bed, I grab her hand to pull her up to her feet in front of me. "Come on then, let me feed you."


As we come down the stairs, I find Jacob sitting on the couch. He looks up as we hit the bottom of the stairs.

"We are going to go grab something to eat, do you want to join us?" I sign.

I watch as he looks behind me and Jayden. "Ms. Edwards, I'm sorry for what I said to you the other day," he signs.

"It's all right, Jacob, I understand," I hear her say behind me.

She is letting him off too easy I think, but I'm not going to push it tonight. He apologized, I am going to be happy about that.

"So did you want to go?" I sign once again.

I watch as he looks between Jayden and myself, then shakes his head no. "I had pizza at Tyler's before I came home."

"All right, I'll be home later then. If you need anything, text me."

He nods and then looks back down at his phone.

When I look back at Jayden, I see the concern in her eyes. She doesn't miss the looks from Jacob, which they are hard to miss. He did apologize but his face speaks of his concerns and disapproval of the two of us. He is going to have to get used to it.

"Jayden, he will be fine, don't worry." I grab her hand and lead her out of the house.

I was expecting some issues from Jacob Monday morning but there were none. He was up and ready in plenty of time. He almost seemed happy to be going back to school.

An hour after school starts, my phone goes off with a text from him. Maybe he isn't ready to go back to school? I let go of the breath I am holding when I read it and all he wants is for me to come down to the school and sign forms for track that the coach needs. He is putting himself back into sports, this has to be a good thing.

I have no idea what Mr. Colter said to my brother, but it completely turned him around. Not only are there no more issues with going back to school, he is going back to sports as well. I need to call Mr. Colter and tell him thank you.

Walking down the hallway of the school, I look into each class as I pass wondering which room is Jayden's. I almost asked the coach before I left, but then thought better of it. I don't want to cause problems for Jayden.

I have just passed a row of rooms and am getting ready to go out the door, when I hear Jayden's voice behind me.

"Cameron."

I turn to see her standing in the doorway of one of the rooms. "Hey, I was just wondering which one of these rooms you might be in." I make my way back over to her.

She points up above the door, it reads Room 12. "This would be mine. I saw you pass by, is everything all right with Jacob?"

She is always concerned about him, even after he has been a jerk to her. He doesn't deserve her worry after the way he treated her.

"Yeah, everything is good. He wants to get back on the track team, I had to sign some papers."

The lights flash through the hallway and before you know it, all the kids are piling into the hall all heading in different directions. I watch as she says goodbye to the kids from her class and when she looks up at me, I notice her looking past me to something or someone behind me. When I look over my shoulder, I see another teacher around Jayden's age standing at the last door of the hallway.

Jayden speaking brings my attention back around to her. "Are you by any chance interested in maybe going on a double date? I would like for you to meet Charliee. She has just started dating one of the firefighters who helped with the rescue."

Jayden had mentioned before that her friend was there that night of the bombing as well.

"I don't know, Jayden. I'm pretty busy with both tracks getting ready to be finished here real soon, time isn't something I have a lot of extra right now."

I try to keep eye contact with her but can't and she is seeing right through my crap, I can see it in her eyes.

"Cameron, what's going on?"

"Jayden, I really don't want to talk about this now or here."

"What's the problem? If we are going to do this, you should meet one of the most important people in my life."

"Jayden, what part of I don't want to discuss this right now was I not clear on?" I know the tone in my voice is harsh, and I shouldn't be talking this way but she isn't letting up.

"Is it because she was involved that night?"

"Jayden, enough!" I hiss at her, trying to keep my temper at bay. I need to leave before I say something I am going to regret. I don't wait to give her a chance to say anything else, I turn and walk away from her. Jayden is pissed and honestly, I can't blame her, but I don't want to talk about this in the middle of a hallway in the school with people all around. Right now I need air.

# CHAPTER SIXTEEN

Jayden

Cameron just walked away from me, what the hell? He isn't even willing to talk to me about this. I know I'm new at this relationship thing, I haven't had a lot of experience with them at all, but I'm pretty sure if the guy you're seeing won't meet your best friends, that can't be a good thing.

I watch until the door closes behind him and Charliee starts walking up to me. How am I supposed to explain this to her? I can see the questions in her eyes as she nears me. This is going to be fun.

"Are you ready for lunch?"

No twenty questions, really? What happened to my best friend? I know she's curious, it's written all over her face. However, I'm not going to push my luck, I let the conversation go for now.

"Yeah, let me go and grab my lunch."

I'm not hungry, thanks to Cameron.

"So when are you going to tell me who the guy was?" Charliee finally asks the question I have been waiting for her to ask.

I can't keep this from her any longer. We are best friends, we tell each other everything. I followed her in shower to get the story about her and Travis.

I take a deep breath. "That was Cameron Tovaren."

Charliee's eyes get large. "How is he related?"

"Cameron is their oldest son. He moved back to take care of Jacob."

"You guys seemed to be arguing."

It isn't a question, Charliee is great at reading situations. I just nod my head.

"What were you two arguing about?"

"It was nothing really."

She studies me for a moment, she knows I'm holding something from her.

"Were you guys arguing over Jacob?" she asks when I don't say anything.

Oh, how I wish that was what it was about. That would be easier than telling her he didn't want to meet her.

"How close have you two become?"

Again, words aren't needed, she is reading all of the answers from my face.

"How long, Jayden?"

"We met about two weeks after the bombing. Jacob had taken a few weeks off from school. They didn't want him to fall behind, I told Cameron I would tutor Jacob while he was out. I ended up going to the house to tutor him. After a couple of times, Cameron asked me out for drinks. He said he needed someone to talk to, so I accepted. He's a great guy, we have a lot of chemistry. Things are great as long as I don't interfere or say anything about Jacob."

"So you guys were arguing about Jacob?"

Right now, I wish I could say yes. "Today surprisingly wasn't about Jacob."

I take a deep breath, I can't keep all of this from her any longer.

"Charliee, the other day when we were getting our toes done, you mentioned double dating. I asked Cameron about getting together with you and Travis. That would be what we were arguing about. It's you!"

"Wait, what?" You can see the shock all over her face, I know she wasn't expecting that answer.

I hold up my hands before she can say anything. "Let me explain."

"Please do," she signs only.

Charliee usually talks when she signs, but when she is mad or frustrated, she only signs. I think she messes up words more during those times so she just reverts to what she doesn't have to think about.

"I asked him about us all getting together. He isn't sure if he's ready to meet you."

"I didn't blow up the place, what does he have against me?"

"Charliee, it isn't like that."

The lights flicker, telling us that lunch is over. I don't want her leaving now and being upset for the rest of the day.

Charliee quickly stands up and collects her lunch, then turns to leave. Grabbing her arm, I turn her around to me.

"Charliee, please believe me, it's nothing like that. Cameron has a lot of mixed feelings right now. He needs to mourn his parents, but won't because he is staying strong for Jacob. I think he is afraid that if he meets someone who was so closely involved, it will create or open up those emotions. He refuses to be weak, no matter how much I try to convince him that sadness isn't a weakness. It's not really you, it's what you may open up in him."

I am defending him even being mad at him for walking away from me earlier. I don't want Charliee to be upset either. I'm hoping Cameron comes around and if he does then I don't want Charliee not to like him because of all of this.

I watch as Charliee's face softens a little. She is coming around, I knew she would. Charliee, for one, never stays mad at people, she is always looking for the best in a person. I don't think the woman has a mean bone in her body.

"I understand, you just caught me off guard is all. If he changes his mind or you talk him into going out one night, just let me know."

This is why I love this woman. She always understands and forgives.


After school I sit in the parking lot trying to decide if I want to go to Cameron's house, text him or just go home. Cameron hasn't texted me at all since he left earlier today. The pissed off side of me wants to go home. Is this relationship always going to be about fights and apologies? I know it's common to argue but I'm pretty sure the arguing isn't supposed to be more than not. He needs to talk to me, not get mad and walk away and then think he can just apologize when he cools down and everything will be all right. It is going to get old fast.

Today at lunch with Charliee, I made excuses for him, I shouldn't have to do that.

I can't go home, all I will do was sit there and keep going over all of this and become more pissed off. He may not want to talk about it, but we need to. He can listen and I'll talk but then he will be given a choice on how he wants to proceed with this relationship.

Pulling up to the house, I don't see any vehicles here. Well damn, there went my whole get it all off my chest speech I have been perfecting all the way over here from the school. Now I have to go home and dwell on it.

Just as I'm about to pull away from the curb, I see Cameron coming around the corner in his father's truck. I throw my car back into park and sit and wait. Damn it, my speech that I was all ready to lay into him with is gone from my brain and my nerves are jumping all around. Why does this man jumble everything up inside of me?

Watching and waiting, Cameron pulls into his driveway and is just sitting there. At first I think he is on the phone. I get out of my car and can now see that he isn't talking, he is just sitting there. I walk past the truck and up to the front porch. He hasn't even acknowledged that I'm here. I swear I've been standing here for a good five minutes. Is he hoping I'll just leave? Well, he is going to be disappointed because I'm not leaving and I'm not standing here any longer waiting for him either.

Walking up to the truck, I open up the driver side door. "Are you ready to talk to me yet?"

Cameron shakes his head. I'm about to lose my temper completely until he looks at me and I notice how red his eyes are. He's been crying. Now all my anger is gone, I have to fight the urge to jump onto his lap and wrap my arms around him, letting him know everything is going to be all right.

"Cameron, you need to open up to someone."

"Jayden, I think I'm losing my mind. I can't do all of this."

I close the space between us, my hands going to rest on his thigh. "You need to lean on someone, too, Cameron. You haven't even mourned your parents. You've been dealing with Jacob and the business. Your whole life turned upside down without any warning, Cameron, that's not easy for anyone to deal with."

"Jayden, I've disappointed or screwed up everything lately. I have two developments finishing at the same time in two different states. I can't do anything right with Jacob, it takes his best friend's father to get through to him and then I do nothing but piss you off."

"Why don't we go inside and talk about this, Cameron?" My heart feels like a vice is around it squeezing. Here is this tough, nothing bothers me guy sitting in his truck, broken. How do you help the one who's strength everyone else depends on?

He isn't getting out of the truck. "I went by the cemetery. I think I sat there for two or three hours, but couldn't get out of the truck. It still seems like a sick joke. I still walk in that front door," he points up toward the house, "and expect to see my mom in the kitchen or sitting on the couch and my dad sitting in his office working. I sit in this truck and expect to look over in the passenger seat and see my dad sitting there. I smell him every time I get into this damn truck. It takes my breath away every single time, it's like a punch in the face."

His one hand is on top of mine on his thigh. He squeezes it more and more with every word he speaks. I'm fighting the tears now, but I need to keep them from falling. Cameron doesn't need me crying for him, he needs the strength of someone to lean onto right now.

"This isn't something that you get used to in a couple of weeks, Cameron. It's going to take a long time to feel normal again, if ever. I'm pretty sure you will always expect to see them when you walk into that house. It's home! Your parents were home for you boys, they are part of that house and all the great memories you have of growing up. Talking about them and what's going through your head or maybe even asking for help every once in a while might help. Problem is you are still pushing everyone away who wants to help you. You are shutting everyone out."

He doesn't say anything in response. He just keeps staring at the house, but he does keep the tight grip on my hand. I just stand there and wait. There is nothing else I can say, he has to make the next move.

"I know you are mad at me about today," he finally speaks.

"I'm upset that you shut me out, Cameron. One minute you want a relationship, the next you are walking away from me. If you aren't ready to do something like meet my best friend because it ties into your parents' death, I'm not going to be mad at you. What pisses me off is when you say nothing and walk away from me. I can deal with you yelling at me, before dealing with you giving the silent treatment and walking away."

"I saw her and wondered why my parents died but she didn't. What did she do so different in her life that rewarded her to live?"

I am speechless for a moment. He is trying to figure out what happened in life for certain people to have been taken and others not.

"Cameron, it was timing. Wrong place at the wrong time.

Your parents didn't do something wrong. They were just in the wrong place at the wrong time."

This is the only explanation I can think to give. Aside from being taken back on the fact that he thought his parents did something wrong and that's why they died. I think about it all of the time. If Charliee would have been only five seconds slower about walking out that front door. I am still amazed that she lived through having the entire front wall of the building burying her.

"I'm not mad that your friend lived, I'm just mad that my parents didn't, Jayden. I'm not ready to meet her. I don't have a great excuse, but it will have to be enough for right now."

"There doesn't have to be an excuse, Cameron. I just need to know what's going on."

He finally looks over at me. "I'm not making your first relationship a good experience, am I?"

I can't hold the small laugh from bubbling out. "I'm not expecting only happiness but yes, this has been an experience."

"Are you still wanting to stick around?"

"Cameron, I'm a fighter. I'll be able to handle it all for now. Just don't keep shutting me out."

Leaning forward, he kisses me gently. "How about I take you out to dinner. I know it's not a double date, but it's a date."

I can't wait for him to meet Charliee. He is becoming a piece of my life and she is my other half, but for now I will wait.

"Sounds nice, how about I drive?" I will at least try and get him away from the memories for a few hours.

"We can take your car, but can I drive?" he asks.

"What's wrong with my driving? You have never been in a car with me while I drove."

"I hate being the passenger," he states calmly but with a hint of a smile.

*Smart answer,* I think to myself. He doesn't trust my driving but isn't going to say it. I hold the keys out to him. "Fine, you can drive!"

# CHAPTER SEVENTEEN

Cameron

The last couple of weeks have gone in a blur. It hasn't been perfect, but what in life is? Even after Jacob said he wanted to go back and do track, he ended up not running. I think everything was too much and that's why I didn't push the issue when he told me he had changed his mind. Now with the summer here, maybe he can work on getting the rest of what's going through his mind situated and then by next year, he will want to go back to the sports for his senior year. He and I have been doing a lot better. He still doesn't talk to Jayden a lot when she is over at the house but he is respectful and that is all I am asking for. He even offered to help us today in Jayden's room with cleaning it all out for the summer break, which is where we are at the moment.

It is the last day of school and all the teachers are cleaning out their classrooms. When Jayden told me she would be staying after to finish, I offered to come and help. I am surprised when I walk in and find Jacob helping her. When I ask her about it, she just tells me he stayed after class and asked what she needed help with. I don't ask any other questions than that.

Jayden hands me the last two books on the shelf we have been emptying. "Hey, I have to go down to Texas next week for the finalization of the project I have going on down there. I'm flying there but driving all my stuff back. Do you think maybe you would like to join me?"

I do believe I just shocked her I am guessing from the look I am getting from her at the moment.

"Really, you want me to go with you?"

"Why does this surprise you so much?"

I watch as she shrugs her shoulders and then starts closing the box we have just finished filling with books. "I don't know, you just caught me off guard asking I guess."

Before I can say anything else, the classroom door opens and a small petite blond comes in with a beautiful German Shepherd following her. This has to be Charliee. Jayden talks about her all of the time and about her dog.

"I'm sorry, I didn't know you had people in here with you. I was finished in my room and just wanted to say bye before I headed home. I will text you later," she speaks and signs at the same time.

I am surprised at how well she speaks. Jayden told me she was completely deaf but spoke, I just wasn't prepared for how well she spoke. My parent's had put Jacob into speech therapy and he spoke on occasion, but nothing like this woman in front of me. I have to admit, I am impressed. The whole time she speaks, her eyes go between Jayden and myself. She knows who I am, I'm sure of it.

She turns to leave, that's when I am surprised to see my brother go up to her and stop her before she gets out the door.

"Ms. Brooksman, I would like you to meet my brother," Jacob signs.

Charliee's eyes meet mine, I have very mixed emotions right now and I believe she reads that in me.

"Jacob, what are you doing?" I ask before I think about it.

Jacob walks over to me. He stands my full height. My brother is a man now, not the little boy I wanted to protect.

"You need this, Cameron, trust me. If you are that stubborn to admit it then do it for Ms. Edwards," he signs to me, basically telling me to get over myself.

Before I can respond to anything, Charliee surprises me by walking over to me. "Hello, Cameron, it's nice to finally meet you. I'm Charliee."

I look down at her hand that she extends out to me. I need to get over this. It isn't Charliee's fault our parents were killed that night and she was lucky to survive. I'm not mad at her. I think my problem is more the why, not who died and who didn't. Meeting someone who was lucky to survive, you felt like you needed to talk about it, and I'm not ready to talk about it.

"Charliee, it's nice to meet you."

We shake hands, I hear Jayden take a deep breath behind me and release it slowly. Jacob is right, I should have done this way before now. If for no other reason than for Jayden. This is her best friend, the boyfriend should have to meet the best friend, but I've been too stubborn to put Jayden before myself. No more, she comes first.

"I have one thing to say, I feel I need to anyway, and then I promise not to bring it up again unless you want to. If you ever want to ask questions, I'm more than happy to answer what I can. I'm sorry for your loss, your parents were great people. You are becoming a very important person to my best friend over there," she points behind me, "which means you need to realize I'm going to be around. I gave space because I understand, but we are part of each other and with you being part of her now, I hope we can be friends."

Now I see why these two are such good friends, they are both full of fire.

"If you aren't already busy tonight, maybe we can all get together. Jayden has been bugging me for weeks to go on a double date with you and this new boyfriend she says you have," I offer, surprising myself.

Jayden appears at my side, her arms wrapping around my waist. The smile she is wearing is well worth the decision to step forward.

"Tonight would be great. I'm going to go let Travis know." Charliee looks over at Jayden, "I'll text you in a while and we will plan something."

I watch as Charliee quickly turns and leaves, her dog following close behind. I look over at Jacob. He isn't looking at us but he is smiling, almost a little shyly. Looking back down at Jayden, her smile falls a little, and the question is in her eyes.

"It's all good. I guess I just needed to be forced to move forward," I answer her question.

"I'm so excited, I have been wanting you two to meet. You will love her and Travis is a great guy, I think you two will get along great."

"I'm sorry it took so long."

She stretches up onto her toes and gives me a small kiss,

which surprises me. Usually when Jacob is around, Jayden doesn't even hold my hand, let alone kiss me. Things are changing and for the better, hopefully this will make our relationship smoother as well.

The four of us end up at the beach, around a fire after dinner. Travis and Charliee are nice to hang out with, both very down to earth. Jayden wasn't kidding when she told me Charliee was a ball of energy, she never stops. To top it all off, she brought s'mores for us to have tonight. It brings back great memories of being on the beach with family and friends growing up.

Earlier tonight, before we met up with Charliee and Travis, I told myself I wasn't going to ruin our evening with talk from the night of the bombing. The further we got into the evening, the more questions I found I wanted to ask. Jayden mentioned Charliee had spoken to my parents that night, she was the last one to talk to them really. The fire is calming to sit back and watch, but the more I sit here listening to everyone talk, the more I want to know some answers.

"Can you tell me anything about that night and my parents?" I sign to Charliee. I don't say a word, I still can't find my voice to ask the questions.

Jayden's eyes swing over to me in surprise; Charliee, however, looks over at Travis. He is her anchor, you can see it all over her face. She begins to tell Travis what I said and he stops her.

"I picked up enough to know what he asked. I've been studying," Travis explains to Charliee.

"I'm sorry, that was rude of me. I just wasn't sure if I could find actual words to ask so I signed them, forgetting that not everyone here probably signs," I explain.

Travis waves it off. "Don't worry about it, I started learning the language because all of Charliee's family and Jayden over there would only sign when they didn't want me to know something."

*Poor guy*, I think to myself. He had both of these women to deal with when he started dating Charliee.

"Well, that's good to know now. Note to self, Travis knows sign language now," Jayden says next to me, lightening up the mood a little.

"That's right, no more talking about me right in front of my face," Travis easily teases back to Jayden.

Feeling bad isn't even covering how I feel at the moment watching Jayden and Travis tease with each other. They are friends, she is part of their lives. I didn't want to get to know Charliee, Jayden had to keep this part of her life separate from our relationship, that couldn't have been easy.

Charliee's voice brings my attention back to her. "I'll tell you the same thing I told Jacob when he came to me about a week ago. There isn't much I can tell you that the police report doesn't already cover. I'll do my best, though, I want you two to find some peace with all of this."

"Jacob talked to you?" I ask, completely shocked. He hasn't said a word to me about the whole thing. To be honest, though, I am happy to hear he is talking to someone.

Charliee nods her head. "Trust me, I was just as surprised as you are now."

One thing I have learned the last couple of weeks is I don't have to be the one there for everything. Don't get me wrong, I wish he would talk to me, I still feel that distance between the two of us, but I'm not going to push it.

"I don't even know what exactly I want to know really," I admit. What do I want to know? What am I expecting her to tell me that will help?

"Cameron, I was waiting for my dinner that I had ordered to go when I saw your parents. They passed me when they were following the hostess to be seated. I only got to say hello," Charliee starts explaining to me.

The fire is dancing in front of me. That was my main question. The fire, the explosion, how much did my parents suffer, what did they feel? The tears I can't hold back, just thinking of them suffering and hurting, I can't handle it.

"Did they go fast, or did they suffer?" I finally find my voice to ask.

I watch as emotions run across Charliee's face. The tears spring from her eyes instantly, running down her cheeks.

"I have no memory of that night past the part where I said hello to your parents. I was walking out the front door when the explosion happened. I remember a lot of heat behind me and that's all. I'm sorry. I pray every day for those who lost their lives that night that they all went quick and no one suffered." Charliee looks over at Travis, pleading with her eyes for him to add something that may help.

Travis leans forward in his chair, Charliee's hand tightly in his own. "Cameron, I was one of the firefighters who first responded that night. I don't believe your parents suffered. The blast was centered right there in the dining area, we found no survivors in that area of the restaurant."

It is strange to feel relief rush through me. Thinking of them lying there, hurt, burning and needing help and not getting it in time bothered me more than anything.

"I'm sorry for ruining the evening, we were having a great time," I apologize.

No one is laughing or smiling any longer like we were moments ago. Both women have tears streaming down their cheeks and Travis looks like he would like to know how to help everyone but can't. He looks over at Charliee, helpless and troubled. I'm sure that night wasn't easy on him either.

Charliee finally breaks the silence around the fire. "I know I can't sit here and say I know what you are going through, Cameron. Yes, I may have been part of that night, Travis may have been there and seen all the destruction, but you lost loved ones, and not just one but two of the most important people of your life. Please don't ever apologize for talking about it or wanting to ask questions. I've learned that talking has helped me heal. It's hard sometimes. You wonder if you want to know the answers to certain questions, but keeping it all bundled up will only hurt you and those around you, trust me on this."

Charliee pauses for a moment, looking over at Travis. She doesn't break eye contact with him as she continues, "I know what it's like to have to put the smile on your face and be strong around the people you love to assure them everything is all right. You are the one who went through it all, yet you need to make sure the people around you are healing." She looks over at me once again, "Find that one person, be it Jayden, an old friend, whoever, and talk to them. Believe me when I tell you it will help you heal and it will help those around you heal."

Charliee is amazing. Her strength isn't something many people have. Travis has his hands full with her, I'm sure she keeps him on his toes. It makes me smile a little to imagine an argument between the two of them, I'm sure he doesn't win often. Charliee, this sweet, little petite thing telling you how it is and is going to be has to be entertaining.

"You are one tough woman, Charliee. Jayden has told me about how they found you and about your injuries from that night. I wish I had half the strength you possess. Thank you for answering my questions, I know this isn't easy on you either."

Travis just sits there staring at his woman. He is a very lucky man and he knows it, you can see it written all over his face, he worships Charliee. Jayden brings my attention back to her when she stands up next to me, holding her hand out to me.

"I'm ready to go if you are."

Travis isn't the only lucky one here. I have this fireball next to me and I need to start making sure she knows how lucky I am to have her in my life. This woman has handled a lot of crap from me and I have said things to her that should have had her walking the other way, flipping me off as she walked away and forgetting my name with every step, but no, she always comes back, telling me how it is and to man up.

Getting up, I follow Jayden over and wait as she hugs Travis and then Charliee. "Thank you for the evening. Cameron and I were talking about going to the fair that they have going on down the beach, do you guys want to join us?"

Charliee looks up at Travis. "I have Monday off," he answers her questioning look.

"Monday it is then. I'll text you later, Charliee, and we will figure out all the details." Jayden turns to me.

I walk over and give Charliee a hug. "Thank you. Just for the record, I'm happy to have finally met you. I'm sorry it took me so long."

"Don't apologize, I understand. I'm sorry I couldn't be more help with answering the questions you had."

"Trust me, Charliee, you helped me out a lot tonight."

Jayden leads the way as we walk away. I don't realize how tightly I have been holding her hand until we get to the car and she turns before getting in and looks up at me. I see her rub her hand a little when I let go.

"Are you all right?"

*Am I?* I think to myself. Actually, I think this is the first time my chest doesn't feel heavy. Kissing her lightly, I smile. "I'm good actually. I'm sorry it took me so long to do this, meeting Charliee I mean. Her strength and her advice was good to hear. I've sat around since all of this happened and listened to you tell me all about her. I've wondered why she survived and my parents didn't and I know that makes me a huge jackass. Then I would be mad at myself for wondering why a person didn't die. It was a lot of mixed emotions to deal with. After meeting Charliee, I feel like a bigger ass than before. It was my parents' time to go, and not hers. It's the whole 'Everything happens for a reason' thing I'm starting to believe. I don't do the mushy words thing well, Jayden, but out of all this bad, something very good came out of it. You!"

A single tear springs from her eye and rolls down her cheek as she brings my lips down to hers. This kiss is different, it is saying what neither one of us are ready to say out loud. I am falling in love with her.

# CHAPTER EIGHTEEN

Jayden

It is a perfect evening for the fair, the weather is great, which also means it is very busy. Everyone is taking advantage of a perfect evening on the beach and a good fair. It isn't a surprise we run into someone we know, but what is a surprise is it is Bryce with a woman who he introduced to us as Darryn and her little girl. No one knew about these new girls in Bryce's life I would guess from the look of surprise on Charliee's face. I can see the questions twirling in Charliee's head over all of it. She and her brothers are very close so not knowing who this is bothers her. All introductions and questions that Charliee may have are cut short when Levi, Charliee's hearing dog, lunges out at a crowd of people, knocking Charliee onto her butt.

Levi is a great service dog, he never acts out of sorts. He

never leaves Charliee's side, but right now he is doing everything he can to get away from her and after something, which puts us all on alert. This is the second time tonight, earlier he started growling at a crowd around us. He is barking now, however, and that is not normal, something is wrong. He isn't backing down, no matter what Charliee does and for him not to listen to her, my nerves start up.

"What's wrong with him?" Bryce asks as he goes to Levi and tries to calm him down, but nothing is working.

All of his barking is drawing the attention of everyone around us. He isn't a small dog and you can tell some are getting nervous to be around him. Travis grabs Levi's leash from Charliee and then helps her up off the ground.

"He did this earlier but I brushed it off thinking something spooked him," Travis says, making sure Charliee is all right but keeping a tight hold of Levi.

"Oh my God." Charliee's voice brings all of our attention to her. All of the color has drained from her face, she looks terrified.

I look in the direction she is looking in but I don't see anything unusual. She doesn't answer, but now her whole body is shaking.

Travis shoves Levi's leash into Bryce's hand and stands directly in front of Charliee, concern etched in his eyes. "Charliee, talk to us."

Charliee finally points across the way at one of the children's rides. "That's the guy from the restaurant, the one who ran into me outside. He is standing there in the blue jeans and plaid shirt. He's wearing a backpack."

Charliee's brothers had her come down to the station a few weeks ago after some video they had found led them to believe the guy that ran into Charliee just before she entered the restaurant that night of the bombing was responsible for leaving the bomb. Charliee was the only survivor who had seen him.

Levi's barking catches the attention of the guy Charliee has pointed out to us. Once he looks over and sees all of us staring at him, he takes off running. That completely yells, "Guilty!"

Bryce shoves Levi's leash into my hands. "Call 911, let them know what's going on. You guys get out of here now!" he yells as he starts running after the guy.

"Cameron, take the ladies and head back to the cars. I'm going after him with Bryce." Travis starts to go after Bryce until Charliee grabs his arm.

"Please, Travis, don't. What if there is another bomb in that bag?"

"Charliee, I'm not going to let your brother go alone."

"I'm going as well," Cameron speaks up.

My eyes fly to him now. I'm sure he knows I am asking him if he is crazy without a word being said.

"That bastard is responsible for my parents' death," he answers my unasked question.

I can only imagine what he must be feeling, but if something happened to Cameron, Jacob would have nothing left. I wouldn't have him! The 911 operator keeps asking me what my emergency is. Cameron is telling me I can't stop him with his eyes.

"You three ladies get that little one out of here," Travis yells as he and Cameron take off in the direction Bryce has gone.

Finding my voice finally, I explain what is going on as we all quickly walk back to the parking lot to wait. Darryn didn't stay, she had her little girl with her and wanted to get her out of here just in case something happened. She told us to tell Bryce to call her later to make sure he was all right. If this situation wasn't so serious, I believe Charliee and I would have both shot off a million questions after seeing the look in Darryn's eyes. She cared for Bryce. How had Bryce kept this from all of us and why?

Charliee and I sit in silence as we watch everyone being evacuated from the fair. The police tried to tell us we had to leave. We weren't going anywhere, and after we explained to one of them who we were, they left us alone. However, I do notice we always have one officer very close by. If that is planned or not, it helps calm my nerves a little. I'm pretty sure Charliee never notices they are there. I sit here waiting to hear anything that will tell me if things went very wrong. Charliee can't do that. Every time I look over at her, I can see her eyes focusing on certain officers. As they are talking into the radios or to each other, she s reading lips—a very useful talent at times like now.

I'm not sure how long we have been sitting here but I am getting restless. I want to get up and go look for Cameron, honestly I am surprised Charliee is still sitting here. Levi quickly stands up from where he is laying down which gets both of our attention. When we look in the direction he is looking, we see Cameron and Travis walking back to us.

Both of us jump up and run to them, launching ourselves into their arms. Charliee speaks first.

"Where's Bryce?" You can hear the panic in her voice.

"He had to stay back, he's fine though," Travis answers her.

"Did you guys catch him?" I ask, but I know the answer the second I look up at Cameron and see the anger in his eyes. I can feel the tension in Cameron's body.

"Where's Darryn? Bryce wanted to make sure her and the little one got home safe," I hear Travis ask.

My eyes don't leave Cameron, he is irritated and tense. He looks everywhere but at me.

"She didn't want to chance anything happening with Kendall here so she took her home," Charliee explains to Travis.

"There is nothing else we can do here, we should all head home." Cameron's angry voice breaks through to all of us.

I quickly give Charliee a hug and when I turn back to Cameron, he has already walked away and is getting into the driver's side of my car. I look back at Charliee to apologize for him not saying goodbye but neither of them seem to care that he didn't so I quickly follow after him. The whole ride back to Cameron's house is quiet. He is shutting down again. When we pull up to the house, he just gets out of the car and leaves me sitting here.

This is crazy. I want to follow him and make sure he is all right but then I think about it for a minute and my anger starts to boil. I understand he's upset, disappointed and I'm sure pretty pissed off, but that doesn't give him the right to act like I'm not here. We are supposed to be a team. Lean on each other when we need an extra shoulder, not shove each other to the side. I am always making sure he is all right. Taking his outbursts and accepting the apologies. Or ignoring it altogether and moving on like nothing happened. I've been sitting here a little time now. He has gone into the house and shut the door behind him. I'm not saying he doesn't need me, but he needs to realize I'm not always going to just be here to be the wall. If I want him to quit pushing me away, I need to walk away and make him come to me. My mind made up, and before I get soft and change my mind, I quickly get out of the passenger side and round to the driver's side of my car.

I've been home for probably an hour or so. Enough time to take a shower and dry my hair. I have to keep myself busy. I wash the couple of dishes I have in the sink. I've even put in a movie and am getting ready to turn it on when I get a text.

**Where the hell did you go?

Really, an hour later he realizes I didn't follow him into the house? Screw him, I'm not even going to answer that question. Where did he think I went? Throwing my phone on the couch next to me, I push play. It goes off a couple more times but I ignore it, I know who it is.

He must have given up, my phone hasn't gone off in a while. I try to pay attention to the movie, not think about Cameron, but it isn't working very well. This is crazy, flipping the television off, I decide going to bed is sounding like a better idea.

I've just started walking down the hall when someone pounding on my front door scares the crap out of me. Whoever it is isn't just a heavy knocker, they are using their fist and pounding on it.

I am getting ready to look through the peephole when the door shakes again from the pounding and Cameron's voice booms through. "Jayden, open this damn door!"

Why is he so pissed off? He left me in the car. Better question, how in the heck does he know where I live? We have only met at his house, he hasn't been here yet.

"Jayden!" he yells again.

Flinging open the door, I yell back, "What the hell do you think you are doing? My neighbors are going to call the cops because of all the commotion you are making out here!"

"I don't give a damn what your neighbors do. Why did you leave tonight? Why didn't you answer my texts?"

He is mad I can see that, but I can see a little fear in his eyes as well. He has been worried. That cools my temper quickly. Now all I want to do is throw myself into his arms, but I need him to understand what he did hurt.

"Would you stop yelling at me?"

Cameron takes a couple deep breaths. When he looks back at me, all I see is relief in his eyes. Before I know it, he grabs me, pulling me up against his body and devouring my lips, all while he walks us both into my house and shuts the door.

Any anger left melts away, along with any resistance. It kind of bothers me knowing that just his kiss can change me so quickly. I can't let him get off the hook this quickly and easily this time. I push away from him and take a step back. He takes a step toward me again and I hold up my hand to stop him.

"Cameron, how did you find out where I lived?"

"I got Travis's number earlier tonight so I texted him and asked."

Crap, now Charliee will be wondering what's going on.

"Don't worry, even due to the fact that I was pissed and worried, when I asked I made sure not to worry them," he answers without me saying a word.

"Pissed and worried about what, Cameron?"

"Really, Jayden? You just left and then when I texted, you didn't answer. I didn't know where you were or if something had happened."

"Wait! You aren't turning this around on me. Did it take

you an hour to realize I didn't follow you into the house, Cameron?"

"Jayden, really, that's why you're mad? Because you think it took me an hour to realize you weren't around?"

"No, Cameron," I am shouting now. "It wasn't that you took an hour. What pissed me off was the fact you closed me out again. I understand you were upset about that guy getting away, but you can't keep putting a wall up in between us. You got out of my car, didn't say a word and walked into the house, shutting the door behind you. It may be just me, but that doesn't say 'Please come on in'. You wanted to be alone, I left you alone."

"Damnit, Jayden..."

I put my hand up to stop him. "No, Cameron, this isn't going to be my fault, so don't start with the whole 'Damnit, Jayden' thing."

Cameron stands there with his hands on his hips. "I have no idea what you want me to say!"

Want him to say? Really?! He really had no clue, did he?

"Cameron, you need to go, there is obviously nothing we are going to figure out tonight. I will tell you this, though, I can't keep being the person you push away. We are together, we are supposed to lean on each other. I understand not everything is going to be smooth, but right now your mood is all over the chart and I seem to be the one you take every-thing out on. I've tried to understand, be here for you when you are hurting, but I can't just be here when you are happy and take the crap when you're pissed. I understand you are disappointed about tonight, but you left me sitting in the car, Cameron. You didn't say a word. You got out, went into the house and shut the damn door, only to finally wake up to the fact I wasn't there an hour later. To top it off, you come here and blame me for all of this. I think that hurts the most."

The anger and fear I saw earlier in his eyes are now gone. Nothing, I see no emotion in his eyes right now. He isn't saying anything, he isn't doing anything, he's just standing there. He is great at being quiet, that is one thing I do know.

For the second time tonight, he turns and leaves me alone without a word. He is walking away from me again. I watch as he turns and walks out of the house, this time he doesn't shut the door. He leaves it open so that I can watch him walk to his truck and get in, driving away without a look back. It is like a scene from one of those sappy girl movies.

Slamming my door, I walk over and grab my phone, quickly typing out a text to Cameron.

**Thank you for proving me right.

Throwing it back on the couch, I don't want to know if he responds or not. I am going to bed, although I am pretty sure I won't be getting much sleep tonight.

# CHAPTER NINETEEN

Cameron

**Thank you for proving me right.

I had heard my phone go off right after I pulled away from Jayden's house, but I ignored it until I got home. Proving her right? I guess I did. I left without saying a word. She did tell me to go though. I'm still trying to get over the fear and worry I felt earlier when she wouldn't answer me. I wasn't used to all this "talk to me" stuff. I didn't want to talk earlier. I was pissed the guy wasn't found. He was so close, he wasn't impossible to capture. The bastard got away, though. The man who killed my parents was there and I let him get away.

How do you talk to someone when the last thing you want to do is talk? What pissed me off more was when I noticed Jayden had left. She thinks it took me an hour to realize she was gone. It didn't! I realized it right away. I actually watched her pull out of the driveway. I realized I just walked in and she wasn't with me. When I opened the door and saw her starting down the street, I grabbed my keys and tried to go after her but she had a head start on me and I lost her. I had never been to her house so I didn't even know which direction she would have gone. I immediately texted Travis and asked where she lived. His first question back was if everything was all right. I assured him it was. Told him we had a little fight, she left and I wanted to make things right. I didn't want to alert either him or Charliee that I couldn't find her and she wasn't answering my texts or calls. He sent me her address. After texting and calling her with no response, my anger started turning into fear. I was worried something had happened to her on the way home and we had no idea where she was.

When she opened her door, I wanted to shake her. All she did was tell me how I was closing down on her again. All I wanted to do was yell at her for scaring the hell out of me. I almost pull back out of my driveway once again and go back, but that wasn't going to do any good tonight, we were both in moods and it would only end up with things being said we didn't mean. Now that I know she is safe at home, we need to both take the night to breathe. I'll call her tomorrow and maybe we will both calm down enough to talk.

Walking into the house, I see Jacob and Tyler sitting at the dining room table eating.

"Did you find her?" Jacob signs as I pass him and head into the kitchen.

I nod and continue through the door, I need a beer. I don't want to talk to him or anyone right now. When I turn from the fridge, Jacob is standing behind me.

"Everything okay?"

Again, I nod as I take a long drink of my beer.

"You guys fighting?"

I'm starting to think I may have liked it when he didn't want to know anything about my relationship with Jayden. Ever since he went back to school, the old Jacob seems to be resurfacing. Don't get me wrong, I am happy about that, I have my little brother back, but right now I want to be left alone.

"Jacob, I'm tired. I'm heading upstairs and to bed."

"What happened tonight?" He isn't letting this go.

I don't want to tell him about the guy tonight at the fair. I don't want to tell my brother that I was that close to the man responsible for turning his world upside down and he got away.

"Nothing major, just a misunderstanding. It will be fine."

He stands there staring at me. I can tell he isn't buying it. I really don't want to see disappointment in someone else's eyes tonight.

"I'm not a child, Cameron."

No, he isn't, but I let him down. "It has nothing to do with you being a child. It's between Jayden and me," I sign.

Again, he just stands there for a moment staring at me. "If you don't wake up to all of it pretty soon, you are going to lose her."

I didn't have time to respond, he turned and walked out. Since when did he care if Jayden walked away from me or not?

If this is the kind of crap relationships are about, I'm not real sure they are for me. Why can't Jayden just understand I'm not ready to talk about it? I'm not wired the way she wants me to be. Grabbing my phone from my pocket, I open the message screen to her name and again read her text.

**Thank you for proving me right.

Right about what? Having a relationship or the way I acted? Here is one problem I have though. If I don't open right up to Jayden and spill my feelings or thoughts, she automatically goes to me putting up a wall and shutting her out. Just having her next to me calms me down. We don't have to talk, I just like knowing she is there. It shouldn't have to always be about talking.

Maybe trying to work on a relationship at a time when my world is spinning on super speed isn't the best idea. It's Jayden though. Even now with wondering if this will work, I can't imagine not being able to call her or touch her. The minute I see her, all I want is her in my arms. That woman does something to me. She has ever since she stumbled into the principal's office. It's not just her looks that draw me to her, it's the challenging look in her eyes, she doesn't back down. She's strong and won't take my crap. She has put me in my spot a few different times. She doesn't show weakness very often but there is an insecurity in her that pops out through her eyes. It makes you want to wrap your arms around her and let her know everything is good.

I want to text something back, but I can't figure out what. Everything I start to text, I delete. I'm just going to wait until the morning. I'll call her or drive over, see if she wants to grab breakfast and talk.

Sleep never happens. I look over at the clock and it reads six-thirty. I can't lay here any longer. The whole night I thought I should have texted back last night and not waited. I almost texted her a few times through the night but didn't want to wake her. Now all I want to do is call her but it is early. I can't wait any longer, we need to talk and not over the phone.

I grab a quick shower and am out of the house. On the way to Jayden's, I stop and grab a couple of coffees and breakfast sandwiches. I would rather talk in private rather than in a restaurant with a lot of people around us. By the time I pull into her driveway, it is eight. Just as I am opening my door, my phone rings, it is Steve. I want to ignore the call but we are at the finish line of the track down there in Texas. If it is something important, I shouldn't make it wait.

"Hey, Steve, what's up?"

"Cameron, just making sure everything is good for Monday. You are all set to be here, right?"

Steve worries too much. He has already called me a least once a day this week to make sure I will be there, it makes me chuckle a little.

"Yes, Steve, everything is good to go. I will actually be flying in Saturday. Since I have you on the phone, are you and your wife free for dinner Saturday night? I would like to take you guys out as a thank you, plus I have a couple of things I would like to discuss with you."

"Sure, not a problem. Wait, is everything all right?"

"Steve, I swear, man, you worry too much." I am laughing.

"It's not worry, it's being prepared."

"No, it's worry, Steve. Everything is fine."

I look up at Jayden's house. "Steve, if that's all, I have to go. Can I call you a little later to clear up any details?"

"Sure, I'll talk to you later."

Hanging up with Steve, I grab the bag with the food and pick up both coffees, take a deep breath and head up to the front door. I knock a couple of times and no one answers.

Should I call and see if she is even home? Her car is here, but that doesn't mean she is here.

Knocking one more time, I step back in surprise when the door flies open. I am met with Jayden, still looking half asleep, glaring at me, wearing a pair of short cotton shorts and a tank top, no bra underneath and her nipples are perked up. It takes everything I have in me not to drop everything I am holding, grab her up in my arms and carry her back to bed, waking her up in a much more fulfilling way.

"Good morning." I smile down at her.

She glares back, then quickly turns away from me, trying to shut the door behind her, but I stick my foot in the way. She doesn't stop so I follow her in and shut the door behind me. I'm starting to believe she is still pissed about last night.

"I brought breakfast." I hold the bag and coffee out to her.

Jayden turns around, arms crossed over her chest. "What do you want, Cameron?"

At least she is talking to me. "I thought maybe we could talk this morning over breakfast."

"So since you are ready, now we can talk?"

Her arms are flailing around as she talks, bringing my attention back to that damn tank top and how little it is hiding. "Could you please go and put on a robe or t-shirt, something? That tank top is doing nothing but distracting me right now.

She looks down at her shirt and when she looks back up, she is smiling, and not angelically either. Her hands go onto her waist, which thrusts her chest out more.

"What do you want to talk about, Cameron, since we seem to be on your time schedule?"

"What the hell does that mean?" On my schedule? Screw the tank top, we need to clear some stuff up.

"Cameron, I tried talking to you last night. You left

without saying a word. However, now you seem to want to talk, so talk."

"Jayden, look, last night I had a lot going through my head. I was trying to sort it all out, including the fact that I let the bastard get away who killed my parents."

"Cameron, you weren't the only one who was going after the guy last night, there were a lot of people who wanted that man caught. My problem last night was you were shutting me out." She crosses her arms over her chest, you can see her temper cooling.

"I wasn't ready to talk. Not just to you, but I didn't want to talk to anyone. I needed to sort things out in my own head first. Just because I'm not talking, it doesn't mean I don't need you or that I am shutting you out. I needed you last night, trust me. Just sitting next to you or holding your hand calms me down, helps me think clear."

For a moment she stands there, neither of us saying a word. After a while, she goes and sits down on the couch, grabbing coffee out of my hand on the way. I sit down next to her, setting the bag with the food in it on the table in front of the couch.

"Cameron, you left me sitting in the car. Walked into the house and shut the door. You never even looked back, you shut me out. There was nothing in your actions last night that said to me 'please stay, I need you with me.'"

"I know and I'm sorry. I actually realized what I had done pretty quickly. When I went back out, you were pulling away down the street. I ran inside, grabbed my keys to follow you but by the time I got into the truck, you were nowhere in sight. It didn't take me an hour to notice you weren't there, I promise. It did take me about an hour to find out where you lived though."

I wait as she stares down at the cup of coffee in her hands. "Jay, look at me."

Her eyes come up, a small smile on her lips. What's that all about?

"I'm sorry. You are right. I shouldn't have walked away from you, but you need to relax a little. I'm not used to all of this relationship openness stuff. I can't even tell you when the last time was that I had a steady girlfriend where I had to worry what was going on between us. I don't talk openly. I deal with it inside my head."

"Cameron, I'm sorry, too. I know all of this is a lot to deal with. You have a lot going on. I remember overhearing my mom one night, honestly I don't even remember who she was talking to. Anyway, she said my father never talked to her. She thought if he had, she wouldn't have been so surprised by all of his actions or maybe he wouldn't have found someone else to talk to."

"You can't keep comparing our relationship to your parents'. For one, I'm not your father. You need to figure out me and how I deal with stuff. We need to have our own relationship, not one based on what happened to your parents or mine."

She rolled her eyes. "I'm trying but if you aren't talking to me then how am I supposed to know?"

"All right, I'm hearing you. We need to work together a little more. You need to quit being so fast to compare what we have with what happened with your parents. I need to learn to communicate more."

"I liked it when you called me Jay."

*I didn't even realize that I did,* I think to myself.

"It's much better than when you call me Ms. Edwards."

"I kind of like the Ms. Edwards. Every time I call you by

160

your last name, you get a spark in your eyes. Almost like a challenge. You become feisty and I like that."

"You like feisty, do you?" She is laughing at me.

"On you I do, it's one of the things that attracted me to you that first day. Are we good?"

She leans over and lightly kisses me. "We are good. Which I'm happy about. When we fight, I don't sleep. It's exhausting."

"How about I take you back to bed, tire you out a little more and then hold you while you take a nap? I'll probably even join you on sleeping. I didn't sleep much last night either."

"Why didn't you get sleep last night?"

There is that insecurity look she gets in her eyes every once in a while. That side of her she doesn't like to show. It is the tough Jayden she likes to make sure people see.

"Jay, trust me, I didn't leave here last night feeling good. I know there are things I did wrong. I hated that you were mad at me. I almost called you a couple of times throughout the night. My parents had a rule with each other. Never go to bed mad. No matter how long it takes to talk it out, you do it before going to sleep. I know why now. You're either up all night fixing it or up all night worrying about it. Might as well fix it."

Jayden puts her coffee down on the table and scoots over to me. "I hate to say that I'm glad you were as miserable as I was last night. I would have much rather been tired because we did this instead."

She grabs the back of my neck and brings my lips down to hers. Her tongue darts in to find mine. I can feel her nipples harden against my chest through that very thin tank top.

"Jay, if you don't stop, I'm stripping you right here and taking you now."

She stands up and I am getting ready to stand up with her to follow her to her room when she quickly pulls her tank top off and lets her small shorts fall to the floor.

"You see, here we can do this anywhere, no one will walk in on us." She smiles down at me, then leans over, grabbing my t-shirt and pulling it over my head.

"Being here will definitely have its advantages." I stand up and remove my boots and remaining clothes as quickly as I can.

Once I am naked, Jayden pushes me back down onto the couch, climbing onto my lap straddling me.

"Just to let you know for the future, I have a spa in the backyard we can use as well."

She lifts her hips and guides herself over my hardness, taking me deep inside of her. Those teasing nipples are now directly in front of my face. I can finally do what I've been wanting to do since she opened the door. Sucking one deep into my mouth, I twirl my tongue around the hard peak.

Jayden moans, her hands in my hair, pushing my face into her chest as she grinds down onto me. My hands on her hips, I lift her up and pull her back down. She is so tight around me that I already feel like I'm going to lose myself inside of her.

Jayden quickens the pace. "Cameron," I hear her whisper as she guides me deep inside of her.

She is close, I can feel her tightening around me more and more with each time that she slides me into her, a little deeper each time. Her movements have become faster and faster. I'm not going to be able to hold back much longer.

I bring one hand away from her hips to her to other breast. I find the nipple and roll it between my finger and thumb.

"Jay, come on, babe, I'm about to lose all control. I need you with me."

I pinch her nipple, suck hard on the other and thrust my hips up. Jayden loses all control. Her body shakes around mine, with each contraction she pulls me deeper and deeper inside of her. Finally, I lose myself inside of her, bringing her breast deeper into my mouth. Jayden calls out my name, tightening her arms and legs around me.

I hold her as she comes down from her release. Our bodies both moist, her head is laying on my shoulder.

"I like it so much more being exhausted like this, than not sleeping because we are fighting," I hear her whisper into my ear.

I laugh. "I agree. You ready for a morning nap?"

I feel her head nod against my shoulder. I gently slide from her, then stand up. "Which way?"

"Down the hall, the door at the end," she answers so low I almost don't hear her.

By the time I lay her down, she is asleep. When I lay down next to her, she turns herself over and lays her head on my chest, her leg over mine. It feels natural, like we have slept like this every night. I have a feeling my bed is going to feel empty from now on.

# CHAPTER TWENTY

Jayden

I have no idea what time it is and I don't care. If I could stay all day in this bed with Cameron wrapped around me or maybe in me, I would. I smile to myself.

"I'm hungry." His deep voice vibrates in his chest against my cheek.

"I'm still sleeping."

"I'll be honest, I wasn't sure if you were ever going to wake up. You snore!"

I slap his chest, rolling off of him. "I don't snore."

Grabbing me around my waist, he pulls me back, my back now against his chest, his hardness pressing against my backside. "I hate to tell you, but yes you do," he whispers in my ear.

His hips move against mine. "Are you hungry or not?" I

ask, smiling to myself. Yes, definitely could stay here all day with this man inside of me.

The pulse in my center starts to wake up. My nipples harden, and my core heats up instantly.

"Food was sounding good earlier, but right now I have a hunger for you," he whispers in my ear. The soft touch of his breath in my ear sends tingles throughout my body.

I turn myself around so that I am facing him, taking his hardness into my hand. I stroke down then up the entire length slowly, running my finger over his tip, spreading the beaded moisture around. I barely touch him and I hear his moan, his hips thrusting up begging for my touch.

"Do I snore?" I tease him with circling my finger around his tip. I hear his sharp intake of breath and smile to myself.

Before I can react I am flipped over onto my back, Cameron's body covering mine, his hardness pressing into my center. He kisses me deeply, my hips thrusting up trying to get him inside of me.

"You snore, and it's not a cute snore," he says, smiling, and then enters me in one deep thrust. My back arches up off bed, taking him as deep as I can.

"No more sleepovers then. I wouldn't want to keep you awake all night with my snoring."

He pulls out and then thrusts deep back in again, my eyes never leaving his.

"Jay, as long as you wake up like this, I'll manage through the snoring."

I slap him against the chest and he laughs which vibrates through my whole body, doing amazing things to my core. I hear myself moan. Cameron's lips claim mine and together we find our release.

"It's almost three in the afternoon. I need food, Jayden."

I must have fallen back to sleep again, Cameron's request for food wakes me up. "Three in the afternoon, really?"

"Yes and as much as I would like to lay here and repeat activities from earlier, I need food. We skipped last night and the food I brought this morning is still sitting in the living room and not sounding as good as it did earlier today."

"What would you like to eat?" Problem is I haven't been shopping and I have no idea what I can make. I wasn't expecting company.

"Why don't we grab a quick shower and I'll take you out to an early dinner. Jacob texted me earlier and told me he is staying at Tyler's house tonight. So we can come back here afterwards and use the spa you told me you have."

"You mentioning the spa is giving me ideas that do not include getting up right now and taking a shower and going anywhere."

Cameron smacks me on the backside and jumps out of bed. "Get up, woman, I need food, you need food, then we will come back and start up on whatever lit up your eyes talking about the spa."

I watch as he walks into the bathroom as though he has been in there many times before. I hear the water go on. Quickly I get up and follow him, joining him in the shower.

"What are you doing?" he asks as he runs my shampoo through his hair.

"Taking a shower." I rub my body up against his.

"We need food. I need food. You doing this isn't helping with getting us out of here and to a food establishment."

I pout up at him. "Are you telling me no?"

He finishes rinsing off. I watch as his muscles flex with each of his movements. How can I need him again? I run my hands down his chest. Before I know what's happened, my arms are pinned above my head and my back is against the wall, Cameron's body pressed hard against mine. He takes my lips in a kiss of pure hunger, and not for food.

His lips move along my jawline up to my ear. "As much as I would love to take you right here up against the wall with the water cascading over your very tempting body, I'll have to restrain myself and settle for food."

Before I can respond, he shoves away from me, leaving me alone in the shower, using my towel to wrap around his waist.

"Hey, that's my towel."

Before leaving the bathroom, he looks back at me. "You didn't grab me one. This one was free." He gives me that cocky smile he gave me the first day we met in the principal's office, the one that almost knocked me onto my butt. "Now hurry up or I'll go without you." Turning, he leaves the bathroom.

We pick a small little diner we all like to eat at that has the best chili fries. Travis's sister had brought Charliee here a while back and she got me hooked. I don't realize how hungry I am until my chili fries are placed in front of me. It's usually enough for two, but I am handling them pretty good on my own.

"Are you still coming down to Texas with me this weekend?" Cameron asks in between bites of his cheeseburger.

"As long as you still want me to go."

"I bought the tickets already so yes, I still want you to go. I just didn't know since everything last night."

"Cameron, I think we both just need to talk more. That will keep last night from happening again."

"I'm not the best at all of that, especially at first. I told you I need to sort things out in my own head first."

Nodding, I know this all now. That's what I meant when I said we needed to talk. Maybe I should say we need get to know each other more. "I know and I understand, but that's what I meant. We need to just learn a little more about each other. I'm sure last night won't be our last argument, but hopefully there will be less of them."

"We will be meeting up with Steve and his wife Saturday night for dinner."

I know Steve is the guy who works with Cameron down in Texas, but that is really all I know. "That's fine, I'd like to meet him. I know you have a lot going on this weekend, I'm going along to help with whatever I can."

The waitress stops by and sets our check down. "Thank you for coming in. Have a good evening. You can pay up front on your way out."

"If you are ready to go, we can go back to your place and try out that spa."

"After what you did to me in the shower, I think you should go home and sleep alone."

Cameron reaches across and grabs my hand, running his fingers over the inside of my palm. Damn him. "Do you really want me to go home alone?"

I feel the tingle from my palm straight to my core. My body temperature rises quickly, and from the look in his eyes he knows what an effect he is having on me. No one is going home alone tonight!

We land in Texas around two in the afternoon. We grab a cab and go straight to Cameron's house.

"It will probably be a little stuffy, sorry," Cameron explains as he unlocks his front door.

He is cute being all worried what I am going to think of his home. "Cameron, stop worrying how the house may look."

He opens the door and stands aside so that I can enter first. Just what I thought, a clean freak. It isn't fancy but it is a guy's place, I wasn't expecting fancy décor. Nice furniture, some pictures on the wall, the simple stuff. It screams Cameron, though. I am impressed.

"You should really dust more often." I turn and smile up at him, teasing him.

Rolling his eyes, he walks past me with my bag. "Get out of my way, or you can carry your own bag."

Laughing, I move to the side and then follow him into his room. This room, just like the rest of the house, is clean, the bed made.

"What are you going to do with all of your furniture since your parents' house is already furnished?"

He looks around then shrugs his shoulders. "Honestly, I have no idea. I'm not sure if I even want to stay in my parents' house, but until Jacob graduates I'm thinking to just get a storage unit for all of it."

"Why not just keep your parents' house?"

"I'm not sure what to do with it, to be honest. I don't think I can change their bedroom, Jacob will be going to college, why do I need something that big? I thought about selling it and getting something else since Jacob will be going off to college."

"What if Jacob decides to go to a local college?"

Again, Cameron shrugs. "I haven't thought much past

getting all of my stuff moved back to Washington, and this place up for sale. Jacob will always have a place with me if he wants it. If we sell the house, he might want a small place of his own. We'll figure all of that out."

The smile is gone. He is pulling back again. He usually does when conversations have anything to do with his parents. It is fine, I'm not going to push anything this weekend. He has a lot to do and worry about in the very short time we are here. We are leaving early Tuesday morning to start heading back to Washington. The drive will take us the rest of the week to get home. We will have plenty of time on that trip to talk.

"What time did you say we were going to dinner tonight?"

"We are meeting them at six." Cameron looks relieved the conversation has changed.

I kick off my shoes and close the space in between us, and unbutton the fly of his jeans. "I think I have a pretty good idea of how to spend our time until then if you would like to hear it."

"I believe I like the way your mind is working, Ms. Edwards."

# CHAPTER TWENTY-ONE

Cameron

"So Steve, there's no way to repay you for everything you have done with finishing everything since I have been in Washington." I look across the table to the man who is tough as nails and would swear he blushed a little. His wife, Carol, just sits there beaming at him. You can see her pride through her eyes.

"Cameron, I wish there was more I could have done to take some of the load off your shoulders. I only met your mom a couple of times but she was a very nice woman. Your dad was a great guy. I'm sorry for you boys' loss." Steve looks a little choked up as he speaks.

My chest tightens for a moment, but I almost lose it completely when Steve looks straight at me and adds, "Your parents would be proud of how well you have done through all of this. I know I'm proud of you."

It feels like a punch to my chest, my breath catches in my throat. Jayden's hand is resting on my thigh and she squeezes it. I grab her hand under the table and squeeze. It helps.

"Thank you, Steve, that means a lot."

It is quiet around the table for a moment. Then Steve clears his throat. "I hope I'm not pushing you, so please don't take this that way, but are you coming back down or what's happening with this side of the company?"

I see a little fear in his face. Steve is worried that I'm not coming back and am going to close this side of things. Now I feel bad that I waited until now to talk to him. He has probably been worrying about this for a while.

"Steve, that's what I wanted to talk to you about actually. I'm sure you know my brother has one more year of high school. I couldn't pull him away his senior year so I have decided to move back to Washington."

I see Carol's shoulders slump a little and her eyes well up with tears. Steve just nods. "Cameron, I figured that you would. It's what needs to be done. I understand."

"Actually, I don't think you do. I have, or should I say we have worked so hard to build this side of the business down here. We have projects lined up. I actually wanted to offer you a partnership with me. You run Texas, I run Washington. We continue to build Tovaren Construction in both states."

Carol's smile can't get any bigger and the sad tears from earlier now spring from her eyes but they are no longer sad tears, they are happy tears. Steve keeps looking around, like he is expecting someone to say "Gotcha" or something.

"Cameron, as much as I appreciate the offer, there is no

way I could buy into half of this company. I don't have that kind of money."

"Steve, you aren't needing to buy anything. I'm asking that you take my spot down here. We can talk all the shop talk later, I just need to know if you are interested. I don't want to lose this side of things, you and I have worked hard and I don't want to see that all go to waste. I know you can handle all of this, we can even look into hiring someone if you think you need the help."

"Hell yeah, I'm interested," he yells a little louder than is needed inside a restaurant. The tables around us all look, giving us curious glances.

Again, it's the good ol' cowboy, and I wouldn't change a thing about him. "That's the answer I was hoping you would give me. Monday before the inspection, we will meet and talk everything over. For now, let's enjoy the rest of this dinner and our ladies."

The rest of the evening goes great. We spend the entire evening with Steve telling Jayden stories about me. It is almost like a father meeting the son's girlfriend for the first time. It is a great night and for the first time in a while, I feel completely relaxed. Things feel like they are finally getting back to as normal as it is going to get, I think. Since the news of my parents, tonight is the first time I am ready to start looking forward again.

I look over to the passenger seat, Jayden is asleep. *Asleep, her feisty side looks innocent,* I think to myself. I know all of this hasn't been easy on her. Not only did she almost lose her best friend, but then she met me. I push a piece of hair off her face. Things with me haven't been easy, I know. Why she has stayed around is beyond me. In each of our arguments, I did see the challenge in her eyes, which was one thing that drew me to her. She gave me that look in the principal's office that first day we met, I think she hooked me from that moment.

After tonight and talking with Steve, knowing he is all on board with my plans of him taking over down here in Texas, I realize it is time to move on with our lives, Jacob's and mine. Our parents would want us to. I know this is going to be easier said than done but it is time. I am ready to work harder on this thing between Jayden and me. My parents would have loved her. My mom always said it was going to take a feisty woman who would challenge me and not take my crap to tie me down. Maybe not in those exact words, but it meant all the same. Jayden definitely did all of that. There is a very insecure side to her, however.

"Hey, are we back at your place?"

I didn't realize she had woken up. "Yeah, we are."

"Sorry, I didn't mean to fall asleep."

"It's no big deal, just means you're comfortable. I'm good with that." I smile at her.

Jayden smiles back, she looks like she could easily fall back to sleep. It has been a long day.

"Let's go inside and get you in bed."

I think she tries to give me her sexy smile but she isn't pulling it off with those sleepy eyes.

"Come on, beautiful, let's go in and get some sleep." Laughing, I get out and round the truck to her side. She hasn't even moved to take off her seatbelt I notice when I open her door.

I reach across and unbuckle her and pick her up out of the truck.

"I can walk."

"You can, but you hadn't even taken your seat belt off yet, you're tired. If I wait for you, we will be out here all night. I

174

don't know about you but I would rather sleep in the bed tonight, and I'm not talking about the truck bed.

"Ha ha." She doesn't fight me, though. Instead, she lays her head down against my shoulder.

Walking straight back to my room, I lay her down on my bed. "Do you want me to change you, too?" I start to pull her boots off.

Sitting up, her second boot falls to the floor. "As much as I'd love to allow you to finish this job, I think tonight I'm going to have to pass."

Laughing at her pouty face, I grab her hands and pull her up onto her feet. "Get changed and we'll go to bed." I watch as she grabs some of her stuff and disappears into my bathroom.

The constant ringing of my doorbell wakes me up. Picking up my phone off the nightstand, it is about nine-thirty in the morning. I am surprised I slept in this long. Six-thirty, maybe seven is the usual for me. Looking over at Jayden, I realize how relaxed I feel. That is until the doorbell starts ringing again. I quickly get out of bed, pulling on my jeans as I walk down the hall.

Who the heck even knows I am home? Opening the door, I hear myself groan. "Candice."

"It's about time you answered the door. What took so long?"

What had I seen in this woman? She looks up at me like she is waiting for me to move, but I keep my stance, my arms stretched out across the doorway casually.

"I was asleep, what can I do for you?"

"Why aren't you letting me in? Aren't you happy to see

me?" She places her hand on my bare stomach but I step away from her touch.

"Candice, I know we have been out a couple times, but that's all it was. I'm sorry. Now if you will excuse me, I'm going back to bed."

I go to shut the door and she stops it. "Do you have someone else in there with you?"

What right does she think she has to even ask me that question? From the look on her face, she is fully expecting me to answer it. I'm starting to lose my patience though.

"I can't see why who I have and don't have in my bed is your business."

She pouts and it takes everything in me not to yell, "Really?!"

"Cameron, you know I love you."

I roll my eyes. I must have had too many to drink the night I met this one. Either that or meeting Jayden has shown me what I want. "Candice, you don't even know me. Look, again I'm sorry, but I'm going to ask you to leave now."

I don't wait for her to respond, I push the door closed, locking it just in case. I wait a minute, I wouldn't put it past her to start ringing the doorbell all crazy again. When I hear a car door slam, I figure it is safe to say she has left. I hadn't dated much, work kept me pretty busy, but I go and find the crazy one.

Walking back into the room, Jayden is still asleep. She must be exhausted to sleep through all of that, Candice hadn't kept her voice down. I am relieved she hadn't come out. Jayden is strong on the outside appearance but very insecure inside. She would ask questions, I would answer all of them but she would play out all kinds of stuff in her head. There is no comparison between the two women, but convincing

Jayden would be a chore I had a strong feeling. Ever since her father cheated on her mother, she thinks that is going to happen no matter who the man is.

I'm not one who normally likes lounging in bed, but looking at Jayden sleeping in my bed, all I want to do is climb back in and wrap my body around her. I quickly strip back out of my jeans and slide back in bed. Jayden stirs next to me, her eyes opening slightly. She has the sheet half on and half off. She is only wearing a tank top and underwear, so I have full view of one very nice leg.

"Hey, what time is it?" she asks in a very sexy, half asleep voice.

I crawl over her, claiming her lips in a good morning kiss. Her body instantly becomes awake. I can feel the heat from between her legs, and feel her nipples tighten against my chest. Her fingers go into my hair, tugging slightly, which makes me harder.

"It's almost ten," I finally answer her.

Her eyes go wide. "Are you kidding?"

I kiss a trail across her neck and then back up to her lips. "I'm thinking of something pretty sweet for breakfast."

Her eyebrows shoot up, but she doesn't move. I begin my journey to her sweetest spot. Her eyes never leave mine as I work my way down her body. Pulling her tank top up and exposing her breasts, I take turns sucking each one into my mouth. As I make my way further down, I slide her underwear down her legs. She kicks them off for me. She watches me with those sexy, half asleep eyes as I work my way down her body to the sweet heat in between her legs.

Keeping her eyes with mine, I lick her and watch as her eyes roll back and her back arches, pressing herself onto my tongue. Her fingers are in my hair, pulling. I about lose it right here watching her. I can feel her body tightening up, she is ready for her release. I think she is about to when she surprises me by pushing me away from her and quickly rolling us over so that she is straddling me. No longer looking half asleep, but fully awake, her hand now wraps around my base guiding me into her very wet, very ready body.

I sit up and Jayden wraps her legs around my waist. Her breasts beg for attention, I suck one begging nipple into my mouth. Her back arches, pushing me further into her, and her hands are back in my hair, pressing her breast further into my mouth. With my hands on her hips, guiding her hips as she rides me and my mouth working on her breast, it doesn't take long for either of us to lose ourselves.

# CHAPTER TWENTY-TWO

Jayden

Since we enjoyed breakfast in bed, we decide to go out for lunch. Today is the only day we have to drive around and enjoy the day. Cameron wants to show me around. Tomorrow, he has to work most of the day with the inspectors and packing up the rest of the house. Cameron is hoping to be on the road back to Washington pretty early Tuesday morning.

We have just sat down and ordered when his phone goes off once again, all morning it has been going off. I notice that he looks at it and then roll his eyes and presses ignore. Then shortly after, he gets a text message and he says something under his breath. He never says who they are from and I don't ask, but it is driving me crazy.

We have just received our food when his phone rings again. "Cameron, answer it. Ignoring it isn't working."

"Fine, I'll be right back." He scoots out of the booth. I hear him answer it as he walks out the front door.

I don't expect him to leave to answer it, now I am even more curious about who it is. He doesn't want me to know, that is for sure. When he sits back down, I can tell he is pissed. I am trying very hard to seem like I'm not bothered but it is difficult.

"Everything all right?" I finally ask after some time of eating in silence.

Cameron just nods. He is shutting me out again.

"Are you sure you don't want to talk about it? You seem pretty bothered by who or whatever it was," I try one more time.

Cameron rolls his eyes and takes a deep breath, but then his attention goes back to his plate of food that he really hasn't touched. I know that look, I have seen it a couple times. Usually each of those times had him telling me to mind my own business and yelling at me, and then me leaving, pissed. We are in Texas, I can't just drive home.

"Never mind, forget I asked," I tell him before he yells or snaps.

Another ten minutes or so goes by and still nothing, I just sit here eating my fries waiting for him to explode. This is crazy, why do I have to walk on glass because he is pissed off at someone else? He either needs to get over it or talk about it, but I'm not going to get the silent treatment from him all day long. He told me he needs some time to think things through before he talks things out. I thought I had given him that time, I mean what could be that bad? I am about to tell him all of that, too, when he finally speaks.

"Look, Jayden, I'm sorry. I think I'm just stressed about tomorrow. I didn't mean to get upset and ruin our afternoon."

"Are all those calls and texts about tomorrow?" I ask, pretty sure they have nothing to do with the inspection. If they would have been from Steve, I don't think he would have ignored them. This is his excuse so that he doesn't need to talk about what is really the problem.

He shakes his head. "No, those are another problem that isn't taking a hint."

Well, if that didn't scream another woman then I don't know what does. My heart leaps into my throat for a second. Then I tell myself to relax. Cameron said I had to stop comparing our relationship to my parents' and he is right. Not every man is a jerk like my father.

Cameron finally takes a bite of his hamburger. "Let's just forget about that and I'll try to relax about tomorrow so that we can enjoy the rest of the day."

So I either push this issue and risk a really bad day, or let it go. Trust that if it's something that I need to know about, he will tell me. In other words, pick my battle. Cameron has really never given me a reason to not trust him, even if it has to do with another woman. I need to let this go and trust him.

"So what were your plans for the rest of the day?" I ask. I watch as his shoulders relax a little when he realizes I am letting it go.

The day hasn't been bad. We drove around and he showed me more of the town. We went by the housing track that he has been working on down here and we went out for dinner. I could tell that Cameron wasn't himself though. He had turned his phone down so that I couldn't hear it when it went off. I saw him checking it every so often, I think more out of making sure Jacob didn't text needing something than any other reason. I didn't bring it up though. I needed to trust him.

When we pull back up into the driveway of Cameron's, I see someone sitting on the porch. It is a woman, all I can make out is she has red hair. Cameron throws the truck into park, cursing a whole string of words. I am about to ask who she is, but Cameron jumps out of the truck before I can, slamming his door shut.

Once again, I am left sitting alone in a vehicle. I watch as he goes up onto the porch talking to the woman. She has her hands all over him and all the while he is trying to keep her from touching him. Now I am getting pissed, why am I sitting here? This lady thinks she can touch my boyfriend? She has another thing coming. Getting out of the truck, I walk up to the house getting ready to give this woman a piece of my mind if she touches Cameron once again.

"Candice, you need to listen to me."

I stop on the step. Candice! I recognize the name right away. This is the woman who Cameron was talking to that day after he first kissed me.

"Is everything all right?" I ask as I walk up to stand next to Cameron. I need to trust Cameron when he told me nothing was going on between them, but it is hard at the moment. I go to grab his hand, kind of claim my status as his girlfriend I guess you could say, but he moves away from my touch. My heart leaps into my throat.

"This has nothing to do with you, you don't need to include yourself," the redheaded woman in front of me spits out.

"Who are you?" I ask, standing my ground.

"I'm his girlfriend," she answers, arms crossed over her

chest. She looks at me like she can't believe I asked her such a question.

I look up at Cameron, he is rubbing his forehead. I wait for him to say something but he doesn't. This woman in front of me looks at me like she is waiting for me to get the hint and walk away. I stand there waiting for Cameron to say something to clear everything up, but no, he just stands there looking down at the ground. Am I missing something here?

"Cameron?" I ask, looking at him, waiting for him to say something.

"Jayden, just go inside." He sounds tired.

I don't care. Did he just ask me to go inside? "Excuse me?"

"Jayden, please, let me deal with this," he points over at Candice, "then I'll deal with this," he points between him and me.

Deal with this? Is he serious, he had to deal with me? Screw him. I'll leave him to deal with Candice. I am pretty sure Candice isn't his girlfriend, but I am done with him. I walk into the house, pulling my phone out of my pocket and calling the first cab company that is listed on the search I found. Cameron won't have to worry about dealing with me next. No matter how much I am falling for him, I am done having him shut me out. Tonight is the worst though. He pushed me aside and for another woman. This woman might not mean anything to him, but that almost makes it worse.

I quickly grab all my stuff, putting everything in my bag as fast as I can. I quickly look up flights, finding one leaving tonight in a couple of hours. I feel the tears burn my eyes, but I'm not going to cry. I won't walk in front of that woman and give her the satisfaction of knowing I am upset because of her.

One last quick look around, I make sure I have grabbed everything. As I am walking back out to the living room, I hear the horn outside letting me know the cab is here already. I hate that I have to walk past the two of them outside to leave, but I'm not going to hide in here until Candice leaves and then have to listen to Cameron yell at me.

Cameron and Candice are both still on the porch when I walk back out. Cameron has a puzzled expression on his face as he looks over at the cab pulled in front of his house. When his eyes swing to me coming out the front door, I know the exact moment when he realizes what is going on.

He grabs my arm as I walk in between the two of them. "Where the hell are you going?"

I look between him and Candice and then back up at him. I can see it in his eyes he has read the situation wrong. He thinks I am leaving because I believe this woman is more to him. He doesn't even think for a second it is because of how he treated me.

"Jayden, this isn't what you think it is." He confirms what I believe he thinks is the reason why I am leaving.

The tears burn once again. I think it almost hurts worse to know that he hasn't figured it out. That his words and the way he talked to me was wrong. I'm not a child, I'm his girlfriend.

"Believe it or not, I'm not upset about Candice. I can see desperation when it's pouring out of someone like it is her."

I hear the sharp intake of breath from Candice but I don't care. I want to turn to her and yell at her, "Yes, I called you desperate," but I control myself.

"Jayden, don't do this right now, just go back into the house."

Why do I always feel like a child being scolded when Cameron is mad at me? "You know what, Cameron? You need to finish up with all your loose ends and business here. I'm going home."

"Jay, don't do this right now," he repeats again.

Calling me Jay almost has me turning back around and waiting for him inside. I take a deep breath, if I give in now this will never change.

"You know what, deal with things here and maybe once you get back, we can talk but right now I need to go home."

I think what hurts more than anything is he doesn't fight harder. I'm not mad, just hurt. I quickly walk down to the cab and don't look back. I don't want to let Cameron or Candice see me cry. There is no holding back the tears this time.

Once on the plane, and I realize Cameron isn't going to stop me, I break down. I wait to see him come running into the airport, stopping me at the boarding area, something. I need to go, I need him to let me go, but I want him to care enough to come after me and stop me. I think I'm a complete mess. Maybe the whole problem isn't Cameron, but me as well. Cameron's problem is communication, mine is reacting without thinking. I jump instead of sitting down and thinking. That is one of the things that keeps me from calling Charliee to come and pick me up at the airport. I sit here and actually think about it. If I call her, she will instantly take my side and get very mad at Cameron. I'm not sure if I want that. I'm not even going to let her know I am home early. I don't want her mad at Cameron. Even leaving him, I can't help but want to protect him.

# CHAPTER TWENTY-THREE

Cameron

"It's all done. Papers are signed, inspection over, out of our hands now. Damn, that feels good." Steve sits back in his office chair and smiles.

I feel a huge weight lifted from my shoulders. I know Steve can handle everything here. He could have handled the inspection without me, but I started all of this with him, I wanted to make sure I was with him to finish it. That was the only thing that kept me here last night after Jayden left. I wanted to run after her, go to the airport and stop here, fly out and go back to Washington, but I had other responsibilities I had to think of.

"Hey, why don't we take the ladies out tonight to celebrate?" Steve suggests, having no idea of last night's mess.

"I have a couple more great stories I thought about to tell Jayden I think she would appreciate hearing," he adds.

"You, my friend, will have to wait and tell those stories at another time." *That's if there is another time,* I think to myself.

"You two already have plans to celebrate tonight?" he asks, raising his eyebrows up at me with that "I know how you guys plan to celebrate" look.

"No, Jayden went home last night."

"Wasn't she supposed to drive back with you?" Steve asks, confused.

I nod, playing with a paperclip on the desk.

"Do you want to talk about it?"

"Not really," I state plainly.

"All right, well then how about you and I head out and grab a final beer?"

"Steve, you act like we aren't going to see each other again. We'll be talking so much you are going to throw your phone when you see my name pop up on the screen."

"Probably but since we saw each other every day here, talking on the phone shouldn't be too bad. Do you want to go for that beer or not?"

I hate saying no, but I am planning on pulling out tonight instead of in the morning. I need to get home and straighten things out with Jayden. "Actually, Steve, I was thinking about starting out tonight so I'll have to take a rain check on that beer until the next time I'm here."

Steve stares at me from across the desk for a moment. I'm not fooling him, he knows why I am in a hurry to leave tonight. I've already been up all night. I watched the taxi pull away with Jayden and I lost my temper altogether. I had been trying real hard with Candice to get her to understand there wasn't and never would be anything between us, but she wasn't letting up. After Jayden pulled away, I came unglued. I am now pissed at Candice, Jayden and myself. I was trying to handle the whole situation without hurting anyone, but I obviously didn't do it right. I think I may have screwed everything up completely with Jayden this time. I saw the look in her eyes, it was that look that kept me from sleeping all night.

"Cameron! Hey, are you all right?" Steve breaks through my thoughts.

"Sorry, I didn't get much sleep last night. I think between that and everything today, I'm just tired."

"And you think driving tonight is a good idea? Why don't you get some rest tonight and pull out early in the morning? You can't make things better if you don't make it to Washington alive."

The dad side of Steve is coming out, I smile. "I won't sleep anyway."

"I was going to let it drop but now I can't. What's going on with Jayden? Obviously she didn't leave on a good note last night."

Pulling the paperclip apart, I sit quiet for a moment. No, she didn't leave happy, but I hold on to the part where she said we could talk when I got back to Washington. That is the only thing giving me any kind of hope that I didn't completely mess it all up. I look up at Steve, who is reclined back in the office chair just waiting for me to answer.

"Candice showed up at my house last night when we got home. She was waiting on my porch when we got there. She had showed up yesterday morning and I thought I made it clear I wasn't interested. Then she either called or texted all day long. When the calls stopped, I thought she got the hint, until I pulled up and there she was."

"So what, Jayden thinks you guys are a thing or something?"

I shake my head no. "I think she knows there is nothing going on between the two of us."

Which to be honest, I was surprised about. She is usually so hung up on what her father did to her mom, I figured she would have jumped right to that conclusion.

"I'm lost. Then why did she leave?"

"I think it has something to do with the way I handled everything last night. Long story short, I'm pretty sure it has to do with me getting frustrated and telling her to go inside and I'd deal with her after I dealt with Candice."

After I finally got Candice to leave and I had been sitting down trying to figure out what I had said to piss her off so much, that comment came running back to memory. I don't blame her for being upset, I am pretty mad at myself for saying something so stupid.

Steve whistles and shakes his head. "You made a few mistakes there, buddy."

Throwing the clip onto the desk, I stand up and walk over to the window. "She did say before she left that we could talk when I get back to Washington."

Steve chuckles behind me. I wish I still had the paperclip in hand so I could throw something at him. "I'm happy to see you are finding the humor in this."

Steve throws his hands up in a surrender. "Sorry. Every man who has been in a serious relationship has been where you are now, my friend. We men learn very early we will put our foot in our mouth a lot. I just wish I could have been there when you told her to go inside and you would deal with her after Candice. I'd put money on the fact that Jayden doesn't give a crap about Candice, anyone can see that woman is just needy and desperate, telling her you would deal with her later I'm sure is what got her all riled up."

Steve is laughing and I am getting pissed. "Candice was driving me crazy, I wasn't thinking," I try to defend myself.

"Women don't care what's going on before you speak, they only hear what's coming out of your mouth when you are talking to them. You'll learn, trust me," Steve continues laughing.

I'm glad he is finding this situation funny. I may have lost Jayden because I was trying not to be rude to Candice. I'm not finding any of this funny.

"Learn what? I'm not even sure if I want to try and work all of this out. I have a lot going on right now. I'm not sure what to do with all of this, maybe I should let it go. Let Jayden go."

Even as I say it, I know I'm not leaving it alone. I hate to admit this but I already miss having Jayden here. I don't want to wait an extra night to get home. If I could leave now, I would.

"I don't know who you are trying to convince, me or yourself. I see that look in your eyes, you are hooked. Can't say that I blame you, Jayden seems great."

"Does this relationship thing ever get easier?"

Laughing again, Steve shakes his head. "You learn, trust me."

"Right! Well I'm learning to apologize well."

"That's a start, son."


It doesn't take long to clean up my side of the office here in the portable for the track housing. I make sure to clean out what I can so that Steve doesn't have to take care of all of it. The trailer will be moved to the next site soon. I didn't sleep last night, so I made sure everything was ready to go for the movers to come get all my stuff. I got on the road around six-thirty this morning. I've tried to call Jayden a couple of times but all I get is her voice mail. All of the texts I've sent have gone unanswered. She said we would talk when I got home but now I am wondering if she has changed her mind.

Once more I try to call, and like the last three of four times, her voicemail is what I get. "Jay, I'm sorry. I'm on my way home. Hopefully in the next couple of days you will decide to talk to me when I get home. I know I apologize a lot to you and I keep saying it won't happen again, but I'm a work in progress and I'm sure I'll mess up again if you decide to give this thing between us another shot. Call me back if you want, but if I don't hear from you before, I'll see you when I get home."

Throwing my phone in the seat next to me, I take a deep breath. She will talk to me even if I have to sit outside of her house. Things are coming around to normal again. I want to work on this relationship with Jayden, I don't want her giving up on us. I have a long drive home, lots of time to think, and by the time I reach Washington I should have a pretty good idea on how to fix all of this.

# CHAPTER TWENTY-FOUR

Jayden

It's been a long week. I haven't heard back from Cameron since his voicemail he left the day he left Texas. He should be back in Washington by now, but I haven't heard anything from him. I am expecting him to show up at my front door at any time now. I have to admit, I miss him. I missed him the moment I sat down in the cab to leave his house back in Texas. I haven't answered any of his calls or the texts he has sent me. I know if I do, I will instantly forgive him and right now, I'm not real sure what to do with this thing between us. He will apologize, I will forgive him and then things will go good for a little while, then something will happen and he will take it out on me again. I can't sit here any longer, I need my best friend.

"Since when do you ring the doorbell and not just come in?" Charliee answers the door, surprise written all over her face.

"Since you decided to get a roommate. I'm trying to be considerate. Is he home today? I didn't see his truck."

Walking past Charliee when she moves aside to let me in the house, I head down the hallway. I am curious how much room my friend gave up for her man.

"No, Travis is at work today," Charliee answers, following behind me down the hall. "May I ask what you are looking for?"

I open the door to her spare room and the office. Turning to her, I laugh. "I was checking out the new look to the house. Nothing has really changed except the large television in the living room. I figured you would have had to clean out a least one room maybe for a gym or something."

Charliee laughs. "Bryan from the station has just moved into his own apartment and needed a lot of what we were going to get rid of, so Travis worked with him on everything."

"So how are things going with having Travis here? I haven't heard much from you the last few weeks."

"It's been good. I'm not the only one who's been busy. The last couple times I've asked what you were up to, you had already made plans with Cameron. I'm thinking everything is going good with you two."

Damn, I shouldn't have brought this conversation up. I was just trying to give her a hard time. That completely backfired.

"Jayden, what's going on? Are things not working out between the two of you?"

There is no reason to try and keep everything from Charliee, plus I don't think I want to anymore. I don't know what to do anymore, I mean I came here to keep from seeing Cameron just in case he showed up at my house.

"I don't know. One minute we are great, the next we are fighting." I need my friend. I need her advice on what to do, but I don't want her mad at him either.

"Are you guys still fighting over Jacob?"

*I wish, I think that was easier times,* I think to myself. "Not really since school got out."

"You love him, don't you?"

No reason to hide it from her or try to deny it with Charliee, she will see right through me. "Is it that obvious?"

I watch as she shrugs her shoulders. "I can see it, but then again that's part of my job description as the best friend."

I hear a vibration coming from the kitchen. Saved by the phone. I point to the kitchen. "I hear your phone going off somewhere that way."

"Thanks," she signs as she quickly heads over toward the kitchen.

Charliee is happy, it is written all over her face. I pull my phone out of my pocket. No calls, no texts. Maybe I should just call him. Maybe he thinks that since I haven't returned any of his calls or texts, I don't want to talk to him.

Charliee walks back in holding her phone. "So, you have plans for today?"

I should call Cameron, but maybe he isn't home yet. I'll give it until tonight. If I don't hear from him by then, maybe, just maybe I'll call him. I just shake my head no to answer Charliee.

"You want to go with me down to the station? Bryce just asked me to come down."

Perfect, maybe this will keep my mind off things for a while. "Sure, I will go with you."

It kills me to see Charliee's disappointment leaving the police station. Sure, they had a little more information on the person who is responsible for so much pain. After seeing him at the carnival, I've noticed a change in Charliee and Cameron.

Charliee is a type of person who always looks at the positive, but today you can see Charliee losing hope, getting frustrated. She is getting mad. I can't say I blame her but it is still a different side of Charliee, one I really hate seeing on her.

"You want to grab some lunch?" I ask as we jump back into the jeep

She checks her phone. "Sure, we can grab something. Where were you thinking?"

"How about that hamburger place down the street?"

She nods then pulls out of the parking space. Before pulling out onto the street, she pulls her phone out of her pocket and hands it to me.

"Can you see who texted me, please?"

"Travis," I sign to her. "He is back at the station. Stop by and tell him what happened."

She asks me to text him back that we will stop by the station after lunch. So I do, of course it isn't going to be that boring. If I was dating a hot firefighter, my messages wouldn't be as boring as the ones on her phone. Best friend privileges in full swing working.

As she parks, I hand her back her phone but I can't control the huge smile on my face. I know I look guilty.

"Jayden!" Charliee yells behind me, stopping me as I walk toward the diner.

I turn around with a questioning look, hopefully looking innocent. Although I'd love to know how he responded to Charliee's text.

"Really? That's what popped in your head when I asked you to text him?"

I throw my hands up in surrender. "I was helping you with dessert. Plus, your text sounded boring. I just spiced it up a little."

I leave it at that, turning and heading inside before she can yell at me some more.

Charliee follows in shortly after. I keep my eyes on my menu as she sits down. When she doesn't say anything, I put the menu down.

"So are you going to make good on your promise?" I smile innocently at her.

"Just remember, payback is a bitch."

I blow her a kiss and wink. "I'll bet he got a kick out of it."

After lunch, we head straight to the station. Charliee basically shovels her food in and finishes in record time. I know she wants to see Travis and tell him what happened at the station. Travis calms her in a way none of us can when it comes to anything with the bombing.

Turning on to the street of Travis's station, the engine comes out of the driveway, lights and sirens on. Charliee pulls over, giving them room on the road. We see Travis in the back cab window and as he passes, he signs that he will text Charliee later and that he loves her. I have to admit, I am a little jealous over their relationship. It is always so comfortable between the two of them. That perfect match you hear about, or true love, the happily ever after, that's what Charliee and

Travis have. I don't think they have ever had an argument. Travis worships Charliee. She deserves it, though, she deserves to be treated the way he treats her. Like she walks on water.

I look over and see her hands tightly gripping the steering wheel. I grab her arm to get her attention. "What's wrong?"

She shrugs, but her eyes look worried. She looks back down the street but the engine has already disappeared around the corner.

Charliee looks back over at me. "Do you ever get a feeling like something isn't right?"

"Charliee, you are just freaking out. Between going to the station today and getting all worked up there and them rushing out of here, lights everywhere, your nerves are just going crazy."

Charliee looks like at any moment she is going to drive after the engine, following them onto whatever call they are headed to.

"I have to admit, firefighters are already hot but watching them rush out of here, lights flashing and hearing the sirens, it makes those guys even hotter."

There is the smile I was hoping for. She is calming down. The worry is still in her eyes, but she takes a deep breath and nods her head in agreement with me.


I am looking for a distraction to keep my mind off of Cameron and today doesn't disappoint. We turn onto Charliee's street to find a squad car sitting along the curb in front of her house. As we pass by to pull into her driveway, both of her brothers step out of the car. I am hoping this has to do with us being at the station earlier, maybe some good news from everything, but I am pretty sure they wouldn't drive over here for any of that. Charliee parks the jeep and we both jump out. I come around as Charliee opens the back door to let Levi out. I look over at the boys, this isn't good. I can see their faces from here and all I see is dread and seriousness. They have on their police faces.

"What are you guys doing here?" Charliee asks when neither brother makes the move to approach us.

Derrick looks over at Bryce and then starts toward us. You can tell he is even less happy to have to be the one to do whatever they are here to do.

"Derrick, what's going on? Why are you guys here?" Charliee is losing her patience, I can hear it in her voice, plus she is talking and signing, never a good sign with her. That usually means she is pissed or upset, something. She always leans back onto signing when she is emotional. I think that is because she doesn't have to think when it comes to signing. Plus, it always seems to get her point across a little better. You know that saying "Actions speak louder than words."

I watch as Derrick looks up at the sky, like he is looking for the easy way to say something. I am about to yell at him myself when he finally speaks. "Charliee, there has been another bombing."

A chill runs through my body. Charliee looks over at me. "That must have been where the guys were going when we pulled up."

A puzzled look comes over her face. Charliee turns back to her brother. "There is more, isn't there?"

"Maybe we should go inside, Charliee." Derrick makes a move toward the house, but no one follows.

"Where was it, guys?" Charliee asks, not moving from the side of the jeep. "What are you guys not telling me?"

"The explosion was at an abandoned building this time," Bryce answers, finally speaking up.

Well that is good news I'd think. Why all the seriousness? I am about to ask but Charliee beats me to it.

"Damn it, guys, what are you trying to tell me?"

Derrick walks up to Charliee and I come around to stand next to her. Something is very wrong, I can feel the tension. This isn't going to be good news.

"Charliee, when the firefighters went in, a second bomb went off. Two guys from Travis's department are missing. Travis is one of them."

Charliee looks pale, like she is going to pass out or be sick.

"Take me there." Charliee starts over to the squad car.

Derrick grabs her by the arm to stop her when she starts to walk past him. "You can't go, we don't even know if it's safe or if there's another bomb, Charliee."

"I don't care. You two drive us over there now, or I'll drive myself. Either way, I'm going. Travis needs me."

Charliee turns around and starts back to her jeep, Levi close on her heels.

I put my hands up to stop her after Derrick pleads with me to help. "Hon, what are you going to be able to do there? Your brothers are right, you are safer here."

Derrick is right, there may be another bomb and she doesn't need to be anywhere near there if another one goes off. There have already been two, why not a third?

"Jayden, you are telling me that if that was Cameron out there, you would stay at home and wait for a call?" Charliee challenges me.

Hell no, I wouldn't sit around and wait for a call and she knew it.

"That's what I thought," she says after I don't answer her, but I don't need to, she reads my answer through my eyes.

Charliee turns back to her brothers. "Now, I'm going to ask one more time. Are you going to take me there, or am I going alone?"

I can see the moment when her brothers give up. Bryce opens the back door of the squad car. Charliee runs over, lets Levi in first and then follows him into the back seat. She looks over at me. I can't stay back and worry, waiting to hear from someone on what is going on.

"All right, I'm coming. Someone has to keep you from doing something stupid and you don't listen to your brothers."


When we arrive, I can't believe the amount of emergency vehicles and personnel that are there. The front part of the building is all rubble. You can still make out the front wall and what looks to be maybe where the door was, but you can see all the walls down inside.

After convincing Bryce she would stay back and not do anything stupid, we are all let out of the back of the car. Someone is being carried out of the building, they have found one of the firefighters. We quickly learn it isn't Travis. Charliee just stands there watching the building; Levi, however, won't stop pacing.

I grab Charliee's hand. She looks over at me, tears in her eyes. "He's going to be all right," I try to reassure her.

My attention is brought to where they are working on the firefighter they just brought out. They are shooting off questions to him and checking for his injuries. The good thing is you can hear the firefighter answer the paramedics.

I feel Charliee's hand being tugged away from mine, but I

hear her tell Levi to calm down so I keep my attention on the firefighter, hoping to hear something that I can tell Charliee to give her hope that everything will be all right.

Turning to update Charliee, I panic. She is no longer next to me. Looking around frantically, the only faces I recognize are Derrick and Bryce and they are both deep in conversation with other officers. Where the hell did she go?

Yelling and commotion at the building catches my attention. My heart stops. Charliee and Levi are running in. A thousand images run through my mind. I don't even notice I have started running in after her until someone grabs my arm to stop me right before I get inside.

"What the hell are you doing?" I turn to see Derrick has my arm.

"Charliee ran inside, we need to get her out, Derrick. What if there is another bomb?"

The words that stream out of Derrick's mouth has all ran through my head. Before I know what is going on, Derrick pushes me toward the other way. Another pair of hands are holding me now and I watch as he runs inside after his sister.

"You were supposed to be watching her," Bryce says from behind me. He must be the one that Derrick handed me off to.

I turn around and glare at him. "Do you know your sister at all?" I yell up at him. "I looked away for a minute trying to hear some information for her and when I turned back around, she was gone."

Bryce starts pulling me back from the building. Emotions are running wild through me. I want to pull out of his grasp, run inside and pull Charliee out before anything else blows up. I want to turn around and smack Bryce for yelling at me for allowing Charliee to get inside. I am mad at myself for allowing her to go inside. I want to sit on the ground and cry!

Neither one of us says another word, we just stand there staring and waiting for Derrick, Charliee and Travis to come back out. I can't stand here and wait much longer, I feel helpless. It feels like I have been standing out here staring at the building for an hour, but I'm sure it is only minutes, waiting to hear the boom. I'm not even sure I am breathing.

A bunch of commotion starts going on, and firefighters start running into the building while police officers start gathering at the entrance. What is going on? I look up at Bryce, he has his radio up to his ear as he listens to the chatter. His eyebrows are drawn together as he concentrates on what he is listening to.

"They found Travis," Bryce yells at me, even though I am standing directly next to him.

"Is he alive? Where is Charliee?" I shoot the questions at him.

Bryce just shakes his head. "That's all I'm hearing right now."

The waiting game again. I am getting antsy. I need to know what is going on. Is everyone all right? Every once in a while Bryce puts the radio back up to his ear, but he won't tell me what is being said.

I can't take it anymore and am about to pull my arm away from Bryce and go in myself when I see Derrick exiting the building carrying Charliee, Levi following close behind. He heads straight over to one of the paramedics. That can only mean one thing, she is hurt. A group of firefighters carrying Travis follows out shortly behind them and rushes him directly over to another waiting ambulance. I can't tell from here if he is alive or not.

Bryce and I run over to where they have taken Charliee. Running up, I notice Darryn, the girl who was with Bryce that night at the fair, working on Charliee's leg. Her knee is cut wide open. I look her over to see if I can see any other injuries.

"What the hell were you thinking?" I yell at her. "If you weren't already hurt, I would beat the shit out of you right now." I lay across her upper body and hug her.

"I'm all right, Jayden," she reassures me.

Standing back up, I wipe the tears away. I hadn't noticed I had started crying. My phone vibrates in my pocket. Pulling it out, I see Charliee's mom's name on the screen. I show it to Charliee and then answer it. I don't get to say a word before she starts shooting off questions and crying.

I step away for a moment while I calm Mom down and explain as quickly as I can what has happened. She just keeps telling me that she can see Charliee being worked on by paramedics on the television. The news crews are everywhere. I explain she is all right and where they will be taking Charliee. She tells me they will meet us there.

I turn back to Charliee and am putting my phone back in my pocket when I hear Charliee yell.

"Bryce, the bastard is here!" We both look in the direction that Charliee is pointing.

"Who's here, Charliee, who are you seeing?" Bryce asks, scanning the area.

I start scanning the area looking for someone who looks out of place. I know Charliee says something else behind me but I don't hear what it is. Bryce, walking toward all of the news personnel quickly and talking into his radio, has caught my attention. Along with the guy in a hoodie who takes off running as soon as he spots Bryce coming at him. There are too many cops here, he isn't getting far this time.

I turn back to Charliee just as another firefighter comes up to her. "Charliee, they are taking Travis to the hospital now.

He is breathing on his own, but hasn't woken up. They have no idea the extent of his injuries so they want to get him there quickly as possible."

"I'm going with him." Charliee tries to sit up.

Darryn quickly gets to work on strapping her down to the back board. Smart lady, get her down before she can get up and hurt herself more.

"We need to get you to the hospital yourself and get this leg checked out, Charliee. You need to sit still," Darryn explains to her.

Charliee is about to argue when I cut her short. "Charliee, you need to get your leg checked. I know you want to go, but you need to take care of yourself first. I'll ride with Travis in the ambulance if they will allow it and keep you posted. I have already spoken to your parents, they are on their way. There is nothing you can do until they check him out, so get yourself treated first."

She wants to argue with me and I can't say I blame her. We don't know exactly the extent of Travis's injuries, or if he will make it to the hospital. She, however, isn't going anywhere. Her knee has bone showing out of it and she needs to get herself fixed first. Finally, she lays back down and nods.

"Come on if you are going with him." The firefighter leads me away by the arm.

They have already loaded Travis into the ambulance so I quickly jump in and sit on the bench next to him. Just as we pull away, my phone goes off again. I am expecting it to be Charliee's mom again, but it isn't. It is Cameron. I don't have the time for that conversation right now. I push ignore and slip my phone back into my pocket. I'll call him back later.

I look down at Travis, and my heart hits my feet. He just lays there. I grab his hand. "Come on, Travis, you have to pull through this, you can't leave her now. She is strong, but if she loses you it will destroy her. You are her strength now and she leans on you, please don't let her fall."

My phone goes off once again, but I ignore it. I just sit here listening to the sirens of the ambulance as we are rushed through the streets and pray.

Everything happens pretty quickly once we arrive to the hospital. The staff goes right to work on getting Travis unloaded and quickly taken back to be examined. I am asked to wait in the waiting room while they take him back.

I have just sat down in one of the chairs when the doors open again and in comes Charliee. She isn't saying anything, all I see is her lying there. My heart falls again, what happened on the way over? Jumping up, I run over to them. I look up at Darryn with the question in my eyes.

"Don't worry, she is fine. I gave her something for the pain and to calm her down a little. It knocked her out, which is probably for the better," Darryn explains.

Two nurses and a doctor come over and I listen as Darryn explains to them Charliee's injuries. Like with Travis, I am helpless, all I can do is stand there and watch as they take my best friend back behind the same doors that Travis was taken through. Hospitals are becoming a place I don't ever want to see again.

I wait for Darryn to finish up with the nurse behind the counter and when she turns back around, I ask, "Have you heard if they caught the guy or not?"

She shakes her head. "No, we haven't heard anything. I was about to ask you the same question."

"Jayden!" My name is shouted from behind me.

I turn and see both of Charliee's parents, along with another older couple running into the hospital.

"Have you heard anything yet?" Charliee's father asks.

I give Charliee's mom a quick hug and am slightly taken back when she goes straight over to Darryn and hugs her next. "They just took both of them back, they said they would come out as soon as they have something for us."

"Darryn, what's wrong with Charliee?" her mom asks.

"I'm not sure exactly what is all wrong with her leg, but she will need stitches, that I know for sure, and I'm sure she broke it but we will have to wait until they examine her to let us know if she'll need surgery or not," Darryn explains Charliee's injury.

"You two know each other?" I ask, a little puzzled.

Both Darryn and Charliee's mom look at each other, Charliee's mom answers, "We have been introduced by Bryce. They have been seeing each other," she explains like I should have already known that.

I feel like something isn't being said and I would have asked more questions but the other lady steps forward.

"How is Travis?" I see the tears in the woman's eyes. This must be his mom.

I look between the lady in front of me and Charliee's mom. "Sorry, Jayden, this is Anna and Kevin, they are Travis's parents."

"Oh, sorry. They both just went back right before you guys came in so we haven't heard anything yet. They just told me to wait here and they would come and let us know when they have something to tell us."

"Did you ride over with Charliee?" Steven, Charliee's dad, asks.

"No, I rode in the ambulance with Travis. Charliee was worried about Travis and giving everyone a hard time about not being with him so I rode over with him to calm her down."

"Was he awake?" Anna asks.

I shake my head no. "I'm sorry I can't give you more information. They didn't tell me anything on the way over here."

The sliding doors to the hospital open again and a very pissed off Cameron comes charging in. How did he even know where to find me?

# CHAPTER TWENTY-FIVE

Cameron

I have just walked into the front door from driving since Monday night when my phone rings. It is David, Tyler's dad. I know Jacob stayed with them while I was gone so I have to answer it.

"Hello."

"Cameron, are you home yet? Have you heard about what's going on?"

"I literally just walked in the door. Is Jacob all right?" Fear slices through my veins.

"Jacob is fine. Sorry, I didn't think, I should have told you that before worrying you. I do think you need to turn the television on to the news. There has been another bombing."

I grab the remote and turn the television on. "What channel?"

"Pick any one of them, they are all covering it. Two firefighters are buried in the explosion. They haven't mentioned names of them yet, though."

David isn't joking. It is breaking news. "Thanks for calling. I already texted Jacob that I was home."

"All right, I'll have him text you on what they are doing tonight."

"Thanks." I place my phone on the table in front of me. When I look up, I see Jayden standing with a police officer. I think it is one of Charliee's brothers. What is she doing there? I don't see Charliee. David said two firefighters are buried. Is Travis one of them? I turn up the volume to listen.

The reporter announces that the first explosion happened at the empty building around one. Shortly after, firefighters arrived and entered the building before another explosion went off. Two firefighters had been caught inside the building. One has already been rescued, but no word on the second one.

As the reporter finishes with his update, the camera is quickly directed back to the rescue. The reporter starts going on about a commotion and people being brought out again. An officer comes out carrying what I think is a woman, but it is hard to see. I thought they said the building was abandoned. Why the hell would they be carrying out a woman? She wasn't dressed like a firefighter. Shortly after they exit, a whole crew of firefighters come out carrying what looks like another person. This one has gear on, he must be the second firefighter. I pick up my phone and dial Jayden, it goes straight to voicemail.

I sit and watch for another couple minutes, hoping to catch a little more information on the people involved, but nothing. I am about to turn it off, I am tired of listening to the reporter just stand there repeating everything because they have nothing new, when all of a sudden all the cameras and reporters are pushed aside. Cops fill the area, all running toward the crowd of news crews. After a moment, a rattled reporter comes on air reporting that the cops are in pursuit of a man who they believe is in connection with the bombings.

The camera scans back to the area of where the ambulances are and that's when I spot her. Jayden is climbing into the back of one of the ambulances. She doesn't look hurt, which brings me to believe something has happened to Travis and possibly Charliee.

I dial her number again. It rings this time, a couple of times actually before I am sent to voicemail again. I send her a quick text asking her to call me and then run out of the house. My truck is still full so I jump into my dad's, his smell once again smacking me in the face. My body runs cold, the irony of the whole situation not going unnoticed.

At a stop light, I once again dial Jayden's number, only to be sent to voicemail again. Once in the hospital parking lot, I find the quickest spot I can and then run to the entrance. I immediately see Jayden standing there talking to two other couples and a paramedic. I take the first deep breath since I got home, she is all right.

I don't move from the entrance, I just stand there and watch as she excuses herself from the group and walks over to me.

"How did you know I was here?" she asks as she walks up.

No hi, hello, happy to see you? Just how did I know she was here? Anger is now replacing panic.

"It's all over the news. I saw you get into one of the ambulances, it didn't take much to figure out where you were headed."

She just nods. I want to wrap her into my arms and assure myself she is all right, or maybe shake the crap out of her for not answering my calls.

"I tried to call you but you sent me to voicemail."

"I was a little busy, Cameron."

"You couldn't answer long enough to tell me you were all right?" My voice starts to raise and brings the attention of those in the waiting room to us.

Jayden closes the space between us, but instead of stopping, she grabs my arm and drags me outside away from the eyes of those inside.

When she turns back to me, there is fire in her eyes. Good, we need to have this out. I have been driving for days thinking of nothing but her, only to come home and find her life in danger by the crazy man who killed my parents. She wants a war of words, then I am all in for that.

"Cameron, honestly, I had no idea you were calling because you were worried."

"Jayden, I've call you a couple of times and left you a text. It never crossed your mind that maybe you should call me back? Damn, you could have even just answered the phone, said hi and said you had to go. Anything would have been better than nothing and not knowing what the hell was going on."

"Cameron, right now all of this isn't about you and me! Charliee is injured and Travis, we have no answers on how he is right now. I didn't think a conversation about our relationship was good timing at the time."

Is she being serious right now? She really thinks the only reason I was calling was to talk about what happened in Texas? Unbelievable!

"They are my friends as well, Jayden, and you didn't think

I needed or would want to be here for them? Even if I didn't know Charliee and Travis, I would have wanted to here for you."

She just stands across from me, rolling her eyes, arms crossed at her chest. I am trying pretty hard to remember she is stressed right now, but the attitude I am getting is pretty hard to ignore. I have to keep reminding myself that I am lacking in the sleep department and I have been through the emotions of worry, anger and relief. Neither one of us are in a great spot for this conversation. It is probably pretty safe to say if we keep any kind of conversations going, it won't end pretty.

"Look, I didn't come here to fight or piss you off or anything else. I was worried about you and Travis and Charliee. I'm sorry you thought I would think anything would be more important right now than how those two are doing. Go back inside, I'll wait out here to hear anything and then take off to go home."

I don't wait for her to say anything back. I turn and head back to the truck. I'll admit, I am disappointed when I reach the truck and look back to see she has already gone back inside. Damn, I have never had a woman make me want to shake them as much as Jayden does.

I've been sitting here in the parking lot for almost two hours now when the text from Jayden comes through.

> **Travis still hasn't woken up, but is in a room now. They are done running tests on him for tonight. Charliee had to have fifteen stitches on her knee and has a fracture. Haven't seen either yet. Charliee was wheeled right into Travis's room and won't leave. We

are hoping in an hour or so they will let us in to
see him.

It isn't a lot to go on about Travis but a least he is in a room
now. I'm still a little confused on how Charliee got hurt. I
have questions but I don't ask any of them. Sitting here for two
hours has given me a lot of time to think. It is amazing how
fast life can change. I can't believe how fast mine has changed.
First losing our parents. Coming back to Washington. Raising
a teenager. Meeting Jayden. Bringing Steve on as a partner.
My life went from all work and only having myself to take
care of to being completely flipped the other way and not
having a second of time to myself.

When I first got back to the truck tonight after talking to
Jayden, I had convinced myself I was over trying to make this
thing between us work. I was pissed. How could Jayden think
I would come here at a time like now and be shallow enough
to not be worried about our friends and only thinking about
our little fight? Sure, we have things to talk about. I would
hope she knows me better than to think that is what I thought
was more important right now.

Were things between us ever going to be easy? It always
feels like we would have things going great, but then there
would be that one moment and everything would blow up.
We never just argued and talked things out, our fighting world
usually has Jayden storming away from me and me chasing
her down to apologize. I know relationships have ups and
downs but ours is getting a little crazy. I've asked myself many
times this week and a few times in the last couple of hours
sitting out here if this is all worth it.

Then I think back to this week without her. I hated not
having her with me on the drive from Texas. I would drive

longer than was probably safe for myself and others around me before I would finally pull over and get a little sleep just because I wanted to get back and clear things up with her.

Today when I saw her on the news, my world stopped. Sure, I saw her jump into the back of that ambulance, but I didn't know if she was hurt or if another bomb would go off while she was there. All I knew was I wasn't there to protect her and that was a feeling I didn't like. There are no words to describe how I felt when I entered that hospital and saw her standing there in the waiting room. She was safe and unharmed. I don't think I took a solid breath until that moment.

Then she attacked. Accusing me of being selfish basically. After the first hour of sitting here had passed, I thought about just going home and waiting there to hear how Travis and Charliee were doing. I figured I could just come back later if I needed to. Then I realized that no matter how mad I was at Jayden for thinking so little of me, if something would happen to either of our friends, I wanted to be here for Jayden. I may not be sitting inside with everyone else, but Jayden knew I was here if she needed me.

My phone goes off once more, notifying me of a text.

**Going in to see Charliee. Do you want to come with me?

I have to read it a couple times to make sure I am reading it right. Jayden is asking me if I want to go with her. One thing it does confirm is she does in fact know I am still here if she needs me.

**Go ahead without me. Tell Charliee I'm here if they

need anything. Call if you need or hear anything else about how Travis doing. I'll come and visit them when things calm down. Their family being with them is more important right now.

That was hard! I'm sure me saying no about going in with her has Jayden's mind spinning. She probably thinks I'm still mad at her and sitting here pouting over it. I do want to make sure family can spend all the time they can with the two right now, that's more important than me going in. Before I can change my mind because of worrying what Jayden is thinking, I start up the truck and pull out of the driveway.

# CHAPTER TWENTY-SIX

Jayden

I must have read Cameron's text at least three times. Maybe I thought the words would change if I just kept reading it. He is mad at me. Can I blame him? I basically accused him of being selfish and unfeeling. I'm worried, tired, and if I'm being completely honest right now, very frustrated at Charliee for the stunt she pulled today, and I took it all out on Cameron when he showed up.

When the nurse came in and told us we could go up and see the two of them now, I texted Cameron right away. I knew he was still in the parking lot waiting to hear any news. Travis's and Charliee's parents had all gone up right away. Charliee wasn't leaving Travis's side so they told both parents they could go up together. I told them I would go up after they were done.

We are still waiting to hear more from Bryce and Derrick about the guy who is responsible. Bryce had been able to send a quick text out, but all it said was everything was under control. Hopefully that means they caught the guy. I'm sure it is still going to be a while before either one of them are going to make it here to the hospital. I did send them a text whenever we got any news from the doctors just so they didn't worry.

I am alone in the waiting area now. I'm sure the parents will all be up there for some time. Cameron is out in the parking lot. Maybe I should go out and talk to him, clear things up. Apologize for how I treated him earlier.

Walking outside, I scan the parking lot for his truck. I even walk around a little, but I don't see Cameron's truck or his father's company truck. He left! My heart drops. I think I may have screwed things up pretty good between us this time. I fight back the tears, maybe I should try and call him.

Pulling out my phone, I am searching for his number when someone touches my shoulder from behind. Jumping and almost throwing my phone across the parking lot, I turn to find Karen and Steven, Charliee's parents.

"Jayden, I'm so sorry. I didn't mean to scare you. I called your name a couple of times but you didn't answer." Karen looks at me concerned.

"Sorry, I was in my own head. How is Charliee doing? Is Travis awake?"

Karen shakes her head. "No, Travis isn't awake. Charliee looks exhausted. I'm sure she is in pain, but you know how she is, she won't say that she is. Are you all right?"

Nodding is all I can do to answer her. I am pretty sure she isn't buying it though. Karen knows me probably just as well as my own mom knows me.

Karen searches my face for a moment, but I am relieved when she doesn't ask anything else about it. "Go up and see Charliee. We are going to her house and grab some stuff since she isn't leaving."

"Do you want me to go instead? That way you guys can be here with her just in case anything changes," I ask.

"No, we will go, you go and see her. Travis's parents are back in the waiting room making phone calls to the family with updates. Charliee needs to see you and I'm thinking you need to see her."

*I need to choke her is what I need to do*, I think to myself. "All right, I'll head up. If you need anything, call me. If anything changes while you are gone, I'll let you know."

Karen gives me a hug, Steven waves as they walk away hand in hand.


Charliee has her eyes closed when I walk in to the room. The wheelchair she is sitting in is pushed as close as it can get next to the bed Travis is laying in, her hand holding his. I stand just inside the doorway watching them for a moment. You couldn't have put a more perfect couple than these two together. Both of them are very caring of others and giving. I'd put money on the fact that they have never had a fight. They are a complete opposite couple than Cameron and me.

Charliee looks exhausted. I am about to leave and let her rest when Levi sits up. His movements cause his leash that Charliee is holding to move, which in turn wakes her up. Her eyes instantly go to Travis. She takes a deep breath and sits back in her chair when she realizes he is still asleep. It breaks my heart to see the pain in her eyes. It makes all the frustrations I have been feeling over her risking her own life today just disappear.

She looks over at me, giving me her best effort of a smile. "Hey, how long have you been standing there? Why didn't you wake me?" she signs.

She must be tired if she is only signing. It seems easier for her than talking sometimes. No thinking required, I guess you can say.

"You are tired, you need your rest. Go back to sleep, I'll come back later. I just wanted to check on you myself," I sign back.

She sits there for a moment just staring at me. "What's wrong?"

She doesn't need to hear about my petty problems with my boyfriend when her boyfriend is lying in a hospital bed.

"I'm good. Just been a long day," I sign.

She gives me that look. The one that says, "You're lying through your teeth."

"Don't worry about it. I'll figure it out later. How are you doing?" I try to steer the conversation away from me.

"I'm on some strong pain medications, so the pain isn't that bad right now. I keep falling asleep though."

"You probably need sleep, Charliee. How about I take Levi outside for a small walk, and you get some rest?" I walk over and hold my hand out for Levi's leash.

Charliee just shakes her head no and eyes the chair next to her. "Have a seat."

I'm not getting away from her, so I plop down in the chair. "Really, it's not important right now."

"Jayden, you look defeated. I'm not doing much right now and I need my mind distracted from all of this." She waves her hand between her leg and Travis laying in the bed.

She is talking more now, but still signing, which means she is waking up a little more.

"I think I screwed things up with Cameron pretty good today."

"What happened?"

"I should probably tell you the whole story." I start back at the beginning with what happened in Texas and me coming home early, and then finish it with our fight downstairs today.

"Before I came up here, I asked if he wanted to come up with me to see you guys. He said he would come by later when everything with the parents settled down," I sign as I speak. Charliee looks ready to fall back to sleep, I'm not even sure if she caught much of what I was telling her.

"So you have been home since Sunday and didn't call me with all of this?"

Well, so much for thinking she wasn't catching the story. She is awake enough.

"I didn't want to complain about Cameron and get you all pissed at him because let's face it, you would have taken my side, then clear everything up with him and you be mad at him."

"What else has happened that you haven't told me about?" Charliee asks, looking a little disappointed.

I can't take anymore disappointment from people today. First Cameron and now Charliee.

"Come on, Charliee, you have been crazy busy with your perfect relationship. You don't need to hear about my crazy confusing one."

The confusion and hurt that shoots across Charliee's face makes me want to slap myself. I am lashing out again, like I did at Cameron earlier today. What the hell is my problem?

"Charliee, I'm sorry. That came out wrong."

220

She doesn't say anything. She just looks at Travis, then back at me. She looks around the room. She is fighting the tears.

"Don't cry, I'm sorry..."

She cuts me off. "No, I'm the one who's sorry, Jayden. You're right. I have been very wrapped up in Travis and our relationship. I haven't paid enough attention to what's going on around me with everyone else. You're my best friend, actually more like a sister. I should have been paying more attention. No, actually I should have made you talk to me more. I noticed you've been distracted, not fully yourself. I knew something was going on. I just didn't want to push you. I figured you would tell me when you needed me. I should have known better with the way you are and for that, I'm sorry."

"Charliee, I haven't exactly been calling you with all of the stuff going on either. We have both been distracted lately."

Leaning over, I give her a hug. My heart breaks when I notice she is hugging me with one arm, the other hand still tightly in Travis's. How selfish can I be? Here she is sitting next to her boyfriend, who is unconscious and we have no idea if and when he will be waking up, and here I am complaining about my relationship. What kind of friend am I?

"For right now why don't we concentrate on Travis and you getting better and not my crazy love life?"

She is shaking her head no as I speak. "We aren't going anywhere." She points between herself and Travis. "And you aren't leaving until we have everything figured out, so start talking, my friend, and I mean start from the beginning. If I start to fall asleep, don't take it personally and just nudge me."

# CHAPTER TWENTY-SEVEN

Cameron

I have been driving for at least an hour before I pull into the cemetery. Pulling up alongside the curb, I take a couple deep breaths. I haven't been here since the day I drove here and just sat in my truck. I haven't been up to the area where they are buried since the day we laid them to rest. Walking up to their area, I bend down and wipe off their headstone. Only one, with a picture of the two of them on it. There was never any other thought of two different headstones. My parents meant the world to each other. I remember catching my dad staring at my mom like she was the most beautiful woman in the world when she would be cooking in the kitchen or talking to someone else. Every time my mom would look at my dad, she had a spark in her eye. Their kind of love not everyone finds. They weren't perfect, I'm sure they had bumps in their marriage, they just never showed it to us boys. Sure, they had their little arguments, but I can honestly say I never saw my parents fight.

I remember back when I was probably sixteen or seventeen. We were getting ready to eat dinner. Jacob and I were already sitting at the table, Mom had just brought a plate over of some kind of dish, and Dad had just come in to join us. Before he sat down, he came up behind Mom, wrapping his arms around her and kissing her. Not a peck, nothing deep, just an "I love you for everything you do to take care of us" kind of kiss.

Jacob had signed to me, "Gross." I just laughed, but I remember asking them that night if they ever fought. My dad smiled, gave my mom one more quick kiss on the cheek and sat down. My mom said, "Nothing is ever perfect, hon, but we keep it between us. We never go to bed mad at each other and we always tell the other, or show," she laughed and pointed at my father, "each other how much we love the other as often as we can. You never know what life will bring, you don't want to regret or wonder if that person you love questions your feelings."

I stare down at the picture of the two of them. I find it funny how that is the memory I am having at this moment. I know I've changed in the last few months. Who wouldn't have with all of this? I've never been the emotional kind of guy. Mom use to tell me it was all right to not always be the strong one. Women like to see a softer side of guys sometimes. Lately I feel like a damn time bomb. I feel like everything is being thrown at me and every one of them I'm throwing back messed up or I missed catching altogether.

"I'm a twenty-eight-year-old man who needs his parents right now."

"We always need our parents, there isn't an age limit to that need." The soft voice comes from behind me.

I feel myself jump a little. I had no idea anyone was around. No one was here when I got here. I turn around to find a lady who looks to be about my mother's age.

"I'm sorry, I didn't mean to eavesdrop on your conversation."

I hadn't even realized I had spoken out loud. She is standing in front of two headstones. One looks to have been there for a while. The other, however, is new, along with the plot in front of it. You can still see where the grass was pulled up and set back in place.

She points over at my parents' headstone. "I'm sorry for your loss. The other day when we buried my father, I must have stayed here for three or four hours after everyone left. I couldn't leave, I felt like if I did he would be gone to me forever. I walked around a little and your parents caught my attention. They were young and just from that picture you could tell very much in love."

I am at loss for words. I just stand there staring at the woman.

"I'm sorry, I shouldn't have interrupted or butted in." She starts to turn and walk away.

"Don't apologize." I finally am able to speak.

She turns back to me. "I'm sorry for being rude, you kind of caught me off guard. I didn't know you were there. I'm sorry for your loss." I point down at her father's headstone.

"Thank you. Dad and I lost my mom when I was very young, car accident. My dad was my everything." She points at the newer looking headstone. "I couldn't have imagined losing both of them at the same time." She points over at my parents' stone.

"Yeah, it's definitely a life changer." I turn to look at their picture again.

"My dad used to tell me when I was having a rough day over my mom, to always remember she is never gone. She is with me every day because of the things she taught me and the love she had for me. I may not see her but she will be walking next to me guiding me for the rest of my life. Our parents may allow us to stumble. They have to so that way we learn to stand on our own two feet, but never fall. That goes for them being here physically or in our hearts." She smiles sadly.

I watch as she blows a kiss to each of her parents' stones and then just turns and walks away without saying another word. Turning back to my parents, that's when something my father once told me comes to me.

"Nothing is meant to be easy, son, in life, love or work. You need to work hard to get it and you need to continue working hard to keep it."

The woman's words hit me. "The lessons they taught me and the love they showed."

"I love you guys." I turn and head back to my truck. I know where I am going this time and what I want to say.

This is the first time in a while my chest feels lighter. Funny how people can come into our life, be it for five minutes, a few months or a lifetime, and change everything you are looking at to be more clear. Fighting and loss is never going to be easy, but neither is loving and gain. Learning something from all of it is what it is all about.

# CHAPTER TWENTY-EIGHT

Jayden

I have to admit, talking to Charliee and getting everything out helps a lot. I need my best friend. Why I thought to keep her in the dark about all of this was beyond me. Plus, she always knows how to tell me when I'm wrong. When I tell her I am going home to change and grab something to eat, she tells me not to come back without Cameron. That is her way of telling me to go and apologize, and to not come back until I do.

Reaching the front entrance is when I realize I don't have a car. It is still at Charliee's house. I guess I'm not going anywhere. My phone goes off in my pocket. I am hoping it is one of the boys with some news. Nope, it is my mom.

"Hi, Mom."

"How is Charliee and Travis doing? Would this be a good time to come by? I wanted to give their families room."

"Mom, you are Charliee's family, too, you don't have to wait to come down. Charliee is doing all right. Broken leg, stitches, but not admitted which is good. Travis is in a room but hasn't regained consciousness yet. They are still waiting on some test results. Charliee won't leave his side. She was falling back to sleep when I was leaving."

"I'll wait a little longer then to come down and visit. I'm sure she is exhausted."

I walk outside, the air feels really nice. It has cooled down for the evening. "Actually, Mom, I need a favor."

"Sure, honey."

Looking around, that's when I notice the truck. It looks just like Cameron's. Is he still here? It is pretty dark in the parking lot.

"Honey, are you still there?" My mom's voice reminds me she is still on the phone with me.

"Sorry, Mom. Yeah, I'm here. Can I call you back in a minute?"

"Is everything all right?"

I notice the writing on the side of his father's work truck. The driver side door opens and Cameron steps out.

"Everything is fine, Mom. I just need to talk to someone real quick. I'll call you back in a few minutes."

"Okay, if you are sure everything is all right."

"Yep, everything is fine. I'll talk to you soon. Love you. Bye." I hang up my phone before my mom can say anything else.

Walking over to the truck, I stop a couple feet away. "You are still here!" It isn't a question, more of a surprised fact.

"Actually, I just pulled back in."

He doesn't move toward me and he isn't saying much. I

can't read his expression. My heart falls a little. This isn't going to be an easy conversation, I have a feeling.

"Charliee may be asleep right now, but I'm sure she would be happy to see you."

Nothing, he isn't moving or saying anything. I am going to say what I need to say and then call my mom back to come and pick me up.

"Cameron, I..." Before another word can come out of my mouth, he is right on me, his lips devouring mine. What the heck just happened?

His lips are soft on mine. Nothing demanding about this kiss. It isn't the kind of kiss that makes me want to climb up his body, but the kind that makes me want to melt at his feet.

He pulls away just enough to look into my eyes. "Jayden, I love you."

What?! Did I hear him right? I pull back a little more so that I can see his whole face, but he isn't allowing me to go too far.

"What did you just say?" I can't have heard what I think he just said.

He smiles one of the sexiest smiles I have ever seen down at me. "I said I love you."

Something is different about him. He looks relaxed, calm. Two things that I just realized I have never seen with him before.

"Where were you?"

Cameron laughs. I'm not sure if I've ever heard him really laugh like this before. What is going on? He hasn't been drinking, I think I would have tasted that when we kissed.

"Let's just say I had an eye opening conversation. I met someone I needed to meet," he kind of explains, I guess.

Something inside of me tells me to just go with it. I don't need to ask questions. Well, maybe just one question.

"Does this mean you forgive me?"

"Jay, we have both said things and reacted to things we wish we hadn't. I know the last few months I haven't been the easiest guy to be around and get to know. We have both had a trying few months. I'm not saying I'm going to change overnight. I'm sure I'll still open my mouth and say things I shouldn't, and overreact to situations without thinking first. I will be fully expecting you to tell me where to go when I do and put me back in my place. But, I'll love you deeply through all of it. You are like no one I've ever had in my life and I want to keep you in my life and just to warn you, I'm not letting you decide any other way."

Tears, damn it! I am crying. Cameron runs his thumbs over my cheeks to catch them as they roll down.

"Are these happy tears?" he asks.

I nod yes. *They are very happy tears,* I think to myself. For the first time in my life, I find myself speechless.

My phone vibrates in my pocket. My mom and her timing. "I have to answer this, sorry."

I pull it out of my pocket, but make sure I don't pull out of Cameron's arms. "Sorry, Mom."

"Are you all right, honey?"

"I'm fine," is all I say as I stare up at the man I love in front of me. I am much better than fine, but don't want to get into that with my mom at the moment.

"Are you sure? I'm not very convinced."

I laugh. "Mom, can I call you back later? I'm kind of in the middle of something."

"All right, if you are sure you are all right. I'll talk to you later."

I shove my phone back in my pocket. Looking up at Cameron, I say, "You should have let me talk first. I had a great apology all figured out. I may have even groveled a little."

He kisses me again. "We both have things to apologize for, but I think we need to move past all of it and move forward."

"You know when I was up there talking to Charliee, she told me I had to find you, apologize and tell you how I feel about you before I was allowed to come back. Then she informed me I wasn't allowed to come back without you."

One eyebrow shoots up. "So how do you feel about me?"

"Somehow between the arguments and sarcasm, I fell very much in love with you."

"Really, only the arguments and the sarcasm?"

I shrug my shoulders. "Well, I guess we had a couple of fun times in between there, too."

"Sarcasm, you're one to talk." He pulls me in close.

"I love you, Cameron."

"I love you, Jay."

# ABOUT THE AUTHOR

Tonya Clark lives in Southern California with her hot firefighter hubby and two daughters. She writes contemporary romance featuring second chance, sports, MC, shifters, suspense, and deaf culture—inspired by her youngest daughter.

When not hiding in the office writing, Tonya has the amazing job of photographing hot cover models, coaching multiple soccer teams, and running her day job.

Tonya believes everyone deserves their Happily Ever After!

facebook.com/authortonyaclark

instagram.com/authortonyaclark

bookbub.com/authors/tonyaclark

amazon.com/author/tonyaclark

goodreads.com/tonyaclark

# ALSO BY TONYA CLARK

## Sign of Love Series

Silent Burn

Silent Distraction

Silent Protection

Silent Forgiveness

## Sign of Love Circle

Shift

Fire Within (Coming Soon)

## Raven Boys Series (Written by Multiple Authors)

Entangled Rivals (Book 3 Can be read as standalone)

## Standalone

Retake

Driven Roads (Coming Summer 2020)

## Anthology

Storybook Pub